Cherished By a Boss 2

Written by: A.J. Davidson

**Cherished by A Boss 2**

Copyright 2016 by A.J. Davidson

Published by Mz. Lady P Presents

In Memory of

Michael Marks

**Dedication:**

This book is dedicated to my boys Jarrett and Ashton. Mommy is trying so hard to make you two proud of her. You would think it would be the other way around. Everything I do is to show you guys that you can do anything you put your mind to. Never let anyone tell you what you cannot do. That is one thing you will never hear mommy say. Regardless of where you go in life, just know I am always in your corner rooting for you and pushing you to beat the odds. I love you both with every fiber in my bones, even though they are aching right now as I type this. Lol, I love you, babies. Muahhhh xoxo Mommy

## Acknowledgements:

Yasss! BOOK 4,

This is still really hard to believe. Little ole country/proper Ashley from Columbus, MS is an author now. First, I would like to thank God because without this gifted mind that he gave me I would not be able to hear my characters. Lol! That is a gift and a curse at the same time. Especially, when they start talking to you in your sleep, and you have to get up and write that part down or make a mental note to do it first thing in the morning.

Secondly, to my family who has been a very big support system for me. My husband for putting up with me and my typing nonstop all day long or talking about characters that he knows nothing about. But, he still sat there and listened to the story. My sisters Alicia and Asia, that Asia will make sure she gets my book as soon as it comes out and I love her so much for that. My baby brother Kayin, I love you baby boy, witcho fat self lol. My cousin British; who one of my characters is based off. She is a real firecracker, but I love her to death. We may have our ups and downs, but I promise you that girl will not let nobody mess with her Ashley.

Mama, I thank you for always saying I CAN DO IT. You wanted to purchase a book just so you could take it to work and brag on your daughter. Lol, I gotta make sure I get you that book.

Daddy, I'm doing all I can to make you proud of me. I also have a mental note in my head from you, "NO FREE BOOKS". He says I worked too hard to give books away for free. Know your worth baby girl, and I promise you it's not free.

My last book was dedicated to my grandmothers. My great grandmother passed away a few weeks after my second book was released. Before I left her house, she said how proud of me she was, and she wished me luck with my books. And for that, I will keep on pushing for you Mama Ida, Rest In Heaven I LOVE YOU! Even on the days, I feel like giving up, I will keep going making sure I never let you down.

## To My Readers

I cannot thank you guys enough. Whether you shared a post, purchased a paperback or eBooks, I want to say thank you thank you a million times. Without you guys, I would not be at book 3. Once you finish a book, you come right to my wall and ask WHEN IS THE NEXT ONE COMING, and that alone pushes me to keep going. Thank you. Now I know I have a lot of readers, but I have to shout out the few that I know are gone ask for an invoice for the next book before it is available. Bianca Johnson, Kierra Weaver, Ashley Justice, Avesha Fenton, Cebrone Herrod, Lauren Cole. Natalie Parker Louis (cousin), Ashley Lockett, Victoria Williams, Robert Williams, Ciera Gavin, Johnie Thomas, Ebony

Blount, Taketa Ingram, Nanniah Whittle. Special acknowledgment to Chase Williams, Miguel Valentin, and my FAVORITE COUSIN British Jackson, for allowing me to use them as characters.

### To My Dope Pen Sisters

Trenae', Manda P, and Latoya Nicole, you three ladies have pushed me to get this book completed. It has been plenty, and I do mean plenty, of times where I wanted to give up, but you guys pushed me and challenged me to get it completed. If you haven't read any of their books, you better get them because you are truly missing out on a good read.

Oh, trust me I can't forget about my entire MLPP team. Let's keep grinding and pushing out these dope books. We are under the hottest publisher out, so there's no excuse for us to fail when she is giving us all the tools we need to succeed.

### My Super Awesome Bad Azz Publisher

I can't forget the DOPEST publisher of them all, MZLADYP!!!I love the fact that she can go into teacher mode real quick and teach you what you need to know to make yourself better as an author, to make your brand stand out, and to make your books bomb. She wants you to succeed, so she makes sure she gives you the real. I swear I love her for that. Keep up the great work! You are amazing! Thanks for taking me under your wing!!

## KEEP UP WITH A.J

Facebook: Author AJ Davidson

Like Page: Author AJ Davidson

Readers Group: AJ Tha Pen Pusha:

Instagram:Aj_penpusha

Twitter: aj_penpusha

## Tank

"Tank, baby, please calm down!" British yelled out to me as I threw another glass vase against the wall.

I am trying so fucking hard not to lose it. I'm trying to get past everything with my friend. I realized killing is what's causing me to keep having the dreams. I reached out to the guy who hooked me up with my boss for my assignments, and he refuses to let me just walk away.

I can't stop until I finish out the contracts he already paid me for. I guess it was supposed to motivate me to finish them faster, so he paid me two mil up front. At the time, I was just happy about the money. Having shorties on the way, I was trying to make sure my family was straight, so I took the money. A few weeks after is when I realized hearing gunshots is what makes me reflect back on being in the military.

"B, I gotta get out of this shit one way or another." I took a seat on the bed, and she came over with a glass of water and my pills so that I could calm down.

"Take this and just lay back, babe."

"I'm sorry for making this mess. I will make sure I clean it up before I leave out tonight."

"It's ok baby. I would rather it be a glass vase hitting the walls than me." She started to laugh, but I wasn't in the mood for jokes.

"That's true baby, and I promised not to ever put my hands on you again. I will forever keep my word on that,"

"You said you had somewhere to go tonight?"

"Yes," I replied.

"Where?"

"I'm going to kill my boss!"

I got off the bed and walked away because I knew she was about to come with the bullshit. The truth is, this is something I won't be able to walk away from. Until this man is dead, he will forever have this hold on me.

"Tank!"

Shit… here it comes, I know she gonna try to talk me out of it.

"If you go, I'm going with you!"

I turned to look at her and was in complete shock at what she just said. She has been telling me I needed to give it all up and just pay my boss back but shit, I don't give money back. That shit is considered pain and suffering money, and I earned that shit.

"British, you know you don't have to come right. I don't want nothing to happen to you or my babies. If something happened, I would kill myself."

"I know baby, but I promise to be careful, and I will stay in the car."

"No! It's not a good idea. Just stay here, and I will call you when I leave and call you once the job is done. Deal?"

"Deal!"

She rolled her eyes so hard at me. I know she meant well, but I just can't take the chance of something else happening to her or my babies.

"Don't be mad at me baby, come here." She walked over to me with her lip poking out.

Pulling her closer to me, I grabbed her face and gave her the wettest sloppiest kiss ever.

"I love you B, and I will die if anything ever happened to you." I reached down, rubbing her stomach with one hand and her pussy with the other one. I needed to make her feel good before I just up and left her here worrying about me.

"Hmmm!" She let out a moan as she bit her bottom lip. Her pussy was wet as hell, and I couldn't wait to put my face all in it.

"Take those off!" I motioned for her to take her panties off and lay back on the bed.

When she took her panties down and opened up her legs, I saw that pretty pussy drooling. Her pussy was just sitting there screaming come eat me, and I did just that. I feasted on her until I got tired. I didn't care how many time she yelled out she was about to cum. I was trying to take her soul.

Flipping her over I did just as Jhene Aiko said, 'I ate dah booty like groceries'. We both were losing our minds. She was moaning out cause it was feeling good, and I was praying her ass didn't poot in my face.

I saw that pussy was dripping wet, so I had to get inside of them guts. I slid one hand under her stomach and pulled her up into the doggy style position. I eased my dick inside of her because I knew it was tight as hell, but once I worked my way in, I went into beast mode. All you heard was her ass smacking again my pelvic bone. Every time I pulled back some, she would tighten up her pussy lips and damn near make me buss.

"Shit Tank! Slow down baby!" I heard what she was saying, but I couldn't pull myself out. Her pussy was the softest place on earth, and I wanted to sleep in.

I wrapped my arms around her waist like I was giving her a bear hug from the back and started murdering that pussy. Ramming every inch of my dick inside of her, I started to feel myself about to cum, so I pulled it out and released all over her ass.

"Damn baby, that shit was good!" I moaned out as I fell on top of her.

"If you don't get yo heavy ass off me, I know sum!" she spat back at me.

"My bad baby, the pussy's got daddy knees weak." I laid there for a few minutes before I got up and took a shower. I needed to get my mind right before I left the house.

*** 

My guy told me they have their weekly meeting at this warehouse and my boss man is always the first to arrive. That's until tonight. I will already be inside waiting on his ass. We have never met before, but if this nigga thinks that he can just have a hold on my life like this, he has another thing coming. After I get rid of him, I'm laying my guns down for good.

I made my way inside the building; it was at least another hour before Boss man is expected to come in. So I laid low and held my position until I heard the opening of a door. I stood up with my guns drawn and started firing without hesitation. I didn't want to wait until he had a chance to pull a gun out on me, so I emptied the clip on him, then pulled out my other gun to finish him off.

*POW! POW! POW! POW! POW! POW!*

I walked over to him so I can send another one through his head, to make sure his ass was dead. The closer I got, the more my heart started to race like I was about to have another episode.

"Baaaabbbbby, no no no no no... Fuuuuuuuck!" I screamed out as I pulled British off the ground. "British baby please get up… get up… get up… get up! I shook her over and over again before I pulled her into my chest. "B, I'm sorry, I did not know it was you. Why did you come here B? Baby whhhyyy??!" I screamed out with tears pouring out of my eyes.

I could not believe what I just did. "You have to get up British, you hear me? Baby, I need you to get up, please get up… please get up…" I continued to yell out, but she never did respond.

I was just sitting here holding her with blood pouring out everywhere.

"I told you I wasn't living without you, B." I turned the gun on myself, put my finger on the trigger and stopped as soon as I heard someone come into the door; I pulled my gun back quickly and pointed it at the door.

"What the fuck, Tank what the fuck did you do bruh?" Chase yelled out as he ran over to B trying to help me get her up.

"Bruh, I didn't know it was her, I swear!" I quickly replied.

"What the hell are y'all even doing here, Tank?" he screamed out in a panic while pulling out his phone to call the ambulance.

"I came here to kill." I paused for a second and thought about it. "Wait…What the fuck are you doing here?"

TO BE CONTINUED

# Chapter 1

## Cookie

Today was very dark and gloomy; it seemed like the storm clouds were right above the church. I thought it would be pouring down by the time we made it to the burial site, but it held off for us. Everything was so well put together; the funeral was beautiful, and I made sure she looked just as beautiful. Purple roses here, yellow tulips there— those were her favorite colors. I bought her this beautiful purple dress with yellow polka dots all over it. She wasn't your ordinary woman, so we refused to bury her in something simple. She had a purple casket trimmed in gold, and the vault we are putting her in is bronze with a gold plate on the top, engraved with her name.

With so many family and friends around constantly asking you if you are ok, it makes it hard to lie like you are. Trying my best to keep it together, I would just simply nod my head, yes, only because if I opened my mouth, the tears would surely start to fall. I'm glad Chase and Tank were there to help me get through this;

both of them have been a great support system, not just for me, but for the entire family.

Standing here, I am now the last person by her grave. Everyone else walked off to mingle with family and friends, laughing and taking pictures, like this is a family reunion. However, not me, I was not done saying, goodbye. As they started lowering her casket into the ground, that's when the tears began to fall down my face again.

"Wait!" I put my hand up so they could stop. I wanted to get one of the roses off her casket to take home with me. "Go ahead" I announced, once I pulled the flower off. I turned away as they started back lowering her into the ground, with my face full of tears.

"You gotta pull it together baby, you're out here looking real ugly," Chase whispered in my ear, making me laugh before walking back towards Tank.

I really needed that at a time like this. This man has been here for me every step of the way during this time. He and my dad have become the best of friends, and I'm hoping he doesn't slip and tell my dad what he does for a living. Especially, what part his baby girl play in all of this. He does not need to know his daughter pimp more hoes than Bishop Don Juan.

"Are you ready to go, baby girl?" my daddy asked as he pulled me away from the burial site.

"Yea, Dad, I'm ready! If you don't mind, I'm going to go back to the hotel and lay down. I really don't feel like being around people right now.

"No problem baby, I don't want them at my house too long either. I need me a stiff drink and a blunt," he said, just above a whisper.

"Daddy!" I called out in a laughing tone and hit him in the arm. "Now you know you are too old to be doing that stuff."

"And you know, don't nothing get old but clothes and hair weave, baby girl."

I couldn't do anything but shake my head at him; my daddy is a true character. Now that he is older, he makes it his business to keep up with me and what I have going on in my life. When he met

19

Chase, they instantly had a connection; which I thought was really weird. My dad never ever like any boyfriend of mine. Brandon was never allowed to come with me when I would visit my dad and my mom. I don't know why, but it was something about him my father did not like.

"Bye Daddy, I will call you before I catch my flight out in the morning. I enjoyed my family, but it's time for me to get back to my life. I have to check on these babies of mine and don't forget I am sending for you once they arrive. You may as well go ahead and move to Miami so that you won't be here alone."

"Oh trust me, I won't be alone! You know Ms. Jenkins from across the street?"

"Yeaaaa!" I was almost afraid of what he would say next.

"Well let's just say, cake ain't the only thing she been dropping off; she got good pie too." He winked at me and laughed.

"Now Daddy, you need to cut that out." He leaned in and kissed me on my forehead, and gave me a long hug.

"Ok baby girl, I love you."

20

"Love you more, Daddy." I walked over to where Chase and Tank were standing and got into the limo.

***

Landing in Miami, it was one person on my mind I needed to see. I wasn't thinking about work or shit. I just needed to get to my cousin. We all got inside the truck that was waiting for us and went over to Tank and British's house. At first, forgiving Tank was nowhere around my heart. I mean shit, he practically killed my cousin, but I did understand that it was an accident.

Trust me, when Chase called, I was pissed off and scared as shit. I flew out the next day to check on her. Once I made sure she was good, I flew back home to bury my mother.

That was a hard situation for me to deal with, but I was glad I had three great men by my side to keep me sane. I swear at one point I thought I was about to lose it.

*POW! POW!*

"Baby, get down!" Chase yelled out and threw me to the floor. The truck started spinning out of control before it stopped in the median of the highway.

I screamed as I saw the blood gushing out of the driver's arm. Chase and Tank jumped out the truck, guns raised, but no one was there.

"Chase, what's going on?" I asked in a high pitched voice.

"Babe, I don't know, but I'm about to find out."

They quickly got back in the car, and the driver started weaving in and out of traffic until we made it to B house. I jumped out the truck, and they sped off.

*BAM! BAM! BAM!*

I banged on the door trying to get inside as quick as possible, just in case someone followed us. I don't mind fucking people up, but when you don't know where the bullets are coming from, ain't shit yo ass can do but run.

"Good evening, Ms. Bridges," the maid spoke as she opened the door for me.

"Yea.. Hey, where is British?"

"She's upstairs with her physical therapist. Is everything ok, Ms. Bridges?"

Ignoring her question, I jogged up the stairs bursting into the room only to see it was some man between her legs stretching her out. Thank God I was not Tank, or this guy would be dead on sight.

"Hey, cousin." I waved at her trying to catch her attention, so I could tell her about what just happened. She was so wrapped up into this fine ass man between her legs she didn't hear me come in.

"Hey boo, give me a second he is about to wrap this up, riiiight now!"

I watched as he slid his hand up her leg, gently massaging her thigh muscles. She had on some short workout shorts and a sports bra. He was so close to her pussy, if they didn't have clothes on, you would think they were fucking.

*WHEEEP! WHEEEP!*

I felt a gust of wind whip across my face followed by British's screams. I turned around to see Chase and Tank standing behind me. Chase was leaning against the rails and Tank was removing the silencer from his gun and placing the gun in the small of his back.

"You niggas are nuts for real," I stated, turning back towards British.

"Nah, she had me fucked up thinking it was ok for him to be on her like that, especially while she got my babies inside of her. B, call someone to clean this shit up NOW!!!" he roared, then went back down the stairs.

British pushed the guy off her and called the cleanup crew.

"Did you find out who that was yet?" I asked Chase, referring to the shooting.

"No, but I have someone looking out. I think I already have a feeling who it is, and if it is her, she better be ready to square up like a nigga cause I'ma beat that bitch like she stole something."

# Chapter 2

## British

Tank needs to learn how to control that damn temper of his. Granted, dude was rubbing a little too much but shit, we weren't fucking, and that's all that matters, right? You would think he would have learned from shooting my ass, that he is too careless with the gun. I still have dreams of that night, and the last thing I expected to do was live.

*"Taaaank!" I screamed out as I entered the doors, but the gun was going off so many times he couldn't hear me. I started feeling hot shit go through my body. That last shot in the leg took my whole body down.*

*"Baaaabbbbby, no no no no no... Fuuuuuuuck!" he screamed out as he approached me.*

*I wanted to speak up and say something when he kept saying he was sorry, but no words would come out. I had no business being there, but me trying to be a down ass bitch, I went anyway.*

*When I heard Chase come in the doors, I knew then that he was indeed, the boss Tank was about to kill. In a way, I was glad I intervened, but now I'm lying here in a pool of my blood, struggling to breathe and praying that God does not open the pearly gates to let me in just yet.*

*The last thing I heard was Chase calling 911 before everything faded to black.*

*"Nurse, get that operating room ready; we have to get these bullets out!" I heard the doctor yell out.*

*When I started to come to, bright lights were shining in my face and nurses surrounded my bed. Before I knew it, the doctor injected me with something, and I was out again. I woke up the next day with Tank, Chase, and Cookie all sitting next to my bed. Once Tank saw me open my eyes, he ran to my bedside. I was in so much pain, my body was bandaged up, and they had me on so many pain meds. I kept going in and out of consciousness.*

*Tank fired six or seven shots, and four of them actually hit me. Two went into my right thigh, one in my chest, and the other in my forearm.*

27

"I'm sorry!" Tank spoke up pulling me from my thoughts.

"Tank, you have to learn how to control that temper. What if you would have shot me again? You said hearing gun shots are what makes you have flashbacks well then yo ass don't need to carry a weapon. Especially, if yo ass is that damn trigger happy." I knew that would only make him mad, but shit, it's the truth.

I went into the bathroom to start my water for a shower. I had that man's blood all over me, and it took everything in me not to throw up when he fell on top of me.

Stepping into the shower, I grabbed my sponge and poured my Japanese Cherry Blossom body wash all over it.

"Can I join you?" Tank requested, through the closed shower doors.

"When have you ever asked?"

He pulled the sliding glass doors back and got in with me. We have not touched each other since the incident; my body has just got to the point where it does not hurt when I have to push to take a shit.

28

He slowly started rubbing my body and kissing on my wounds gently. Once he made his way to my ears, my kitty started purring, begging for him to get inside of me. Dropping down to his knees, he used those big ass arms to prop me up on his hands like I was a New York Style slice of pizza and he had to use both hands to eat me. Propping my legs over his shoulders, I inhaled right before he started licking around the folds of my lips. The shower water was running down his face as he made his way to my clit. Once he got there, he did not let up. Screaming out in pleasure, I could no longer compose myself.

As soon as he felt me about to cum, he stopped and lowered me down, easing me on his dick. I knew he would take it slow with me since I was not back to 100 percent yet, but once he got inside of me, he gave zero fucks. Just feeling him tear into my pussy made me go crazy, scratching his back and thrusting my hips up against his.

"Damn girl!" He moaned out while taking one of my nipples in his mouth and bouncing me on his dick with his free hand. That nigga must have fucked the living day lights out of me.

29

The pain brought tears to my eyes, but then it quickly turned into pleasure.

"You gone let another nigga get that close to my pussy again?" he whispered and bit on my right ear lobe.

"Hmmm shit, hell no, baby!" I moaned out in pleasure.

"Tell me you're sorry, you hear me, B? I want you to tell daddy you're sorry." The more he spoke, the deeper he plunged inside of me.

"I'm so sorry shiiiitttt! Baby, I promise it will never happen again. Fuuucccck!!!" I tightly wrapped my arms around his neck for support.

The harder he bounced me on his dick, the harder I came over and over again. Then my body did some shit it had never done before. With one last deep stroke, I started squirting. I was so ashamed because I thought I pissed on him. Again, I had never done it before, but my cousin Pam has always told me about it, but I was not prepared for that shit.

Tank seemed to like it cause once he found that spot, he kept hitting it like he was playing a game called 'How Many Times Can You Make British Squirt'.

"Shit B, I'm about to cum!" he moaned out as he pinned me against the shower wall, he let out a loud moan and kissed me with so much passion.

With one hand on the wall and one on my ass holding me up, he released inside of me. Feeling his dick jerk and his warm nut shoot inside of me always make me cum again.

***

"How have you been feeling?" I asked Cookie as we sat outside on my back porch. While I was in the hospital Tank made it his business to get the new house ready for me. Once I finally had the chance to check the entire house out, it had six bedrooms, five bathrooms, an indoor pool, a gym, and he had me a little woman cave out back. He know how much I love house parties and backyard bar-b-ques so he made sure I had a nice grill out back and a nice patio set. Even though my circle is extremely small, I still want to entertain the handful of people that will come over.

"I've been good cousin, still trying to adjust to working with these damn girls. These hoes be giving me a head ache. I reached out to this chick I met that night yo ass ended up in the hospital so she can start working for me. Not as one of my girls but the way she was handling those men in the club to get me out of there made me wanna put her as on my team."

"Bitch, you gone say, that night I ended up in the hospital. Which time your talking about?" I joked.

"That shit ain't even funny. I'm starting to think Tank's ass is the fucking devil. Every time you are near this man you get hurt."

"Yea, I noticed that shit! Maybe I need to stop following this nigga or something. Or maybe I need to call before I come cause if I don't my ass is walking into the fucking lion's den. That nigga be on one, for real."

"Yea I hear you, you say that shit now, but I bet yo ass still follow his ass," Cookie blurted out, and I swear she wasn't speaking nothing but the truth.

I got that nigga phone so jacked up, that he can't go more than 100 miles outside of Miami before my phone starts going off. When Beyoncé's "Ring the Alarm" starts going off on my phone, I already know to go grab my gun and jump in my car.

Tank got life fucked up if he thinks I'm about to sit here and raise these kids by myself, and he just runs off. On top of that, I'm still recovering from bullets that he put in my ass. He needs to be right here with me, point blank and the fucking period.

"Trust me; I will make sure I am good. Like I said I had learned my lesson with popping up on his ass!"

*"Ring the alarm I've been through this too long, and I'll be damned if I see another bitch on your arm."* My phone started going off letting me know that Tank ass has left Miami. Now, this nigga told me he had a job to do, but that it was close by.

"Sorry, Cook but umm... I gotta go.!" I ran into the house, grabbed my bag that I packed for this very fucking day. I keep that shit pushed to the back of the closet. I got a bunch of clothes that I won't wear and this gun that I had specially made that can go undetected through security. I am not about to play no games with him.

Jumping into my car, I went to the tracker app on my phone to see where he is located now.

"Arizona!" I yelled out as I did the dash to the airport. "Fuck is this nigga doing in Arizona?"

# Chapter 3

## Charmaine

"Swamp really tried to take them out boss lady, but it was someone else there trying to do the same thing. Before Swamp could fire, he had already shot the damn driver." my little brother Swamp said as he took a seat in front of me. When he said he didn't finish the job, I damn near wanted to kill his ass.

"Swamp, tell me how you want to be my hitta, but yo ass could not complete a simple assignment. If you saw it was someone else there doing the same damn thing you were there to do, then yo black ass should have taken his ass out first. Fuck all the dumb shit! You have one more time to get this shit done or I'ma tell mama where all of her thongs went when we were kids. Now get ya lil' gay ass up and get the job done!" I spat,

"Swamp's got you, sis. I'ma holla at you later before you say the wrong thing to piss Swamp off."

"Bye nigga, and stop speaking of yourself in third person witcho dumb ass." I hate when he does that bullshit.

Now, I have to find out who this other person is since his aim is obviously better than my brothers. Maybe I need to get him or her on my team. I will be the head bitch in charge one way or another. I grabbed my keys off the table and decided to do a little digging. My only thought was to go right to the warehouse, where I knew they would be. Jumping in my car, I did the dash over there, trying to get there before the meeting was over. After sitting there for 45 minutes or so, I finally saw them coming out.

I watched as Chase and Tank exited the warehouse with the girls behind him. He got rid of Duchess, so I had to find another informant on the inside to let me know what they are planning, and I have just the right person in mind.

*RING... RING!*

"It took you long enough to call me," I spoke to my new informant.

"You know I had to make sure no one was following me. I'm down for whatever you have in mind. But first I'ma need some of that pussy to keep me motivated."

Pulling the phone away from my ear, I rolled my eyes so hard. Here he goes with this bullshit. I guess nothing in life is free so let me put my big girl panties on and make this shit happen.

"Meet me at my spot in an hour," I said after putting the phone back to my ear.

"Make sure you have some energy, cause I plan on going all night." I clicked the phone on his ass.

Major is fine, but when he walked into the room, my pussy doesn't instantly get wet like it does for Chase. He gone have to eat ass and all to get this nut out for me. Pulling off from the warehouse, I made my way back to my place so I could get ready for Major.

*** 

Lying across my bed watching Major put his clothes back on, I was trying so hard not to like that shit, but hell, Major put that good dick on me and had me change all my thoughts about his ass. Talking about my pussy does not get wet for him how it does for Chase, shiiid I fooled myself. As soon as Major dropped dem draws, my pussy suddenly had a heartbeat. I had to cross my legs and squeeze gently to get it to calm down. He stood a smooth 6'0 feet, skin the color of a Hershey Kiss, chiseled body— his body looked like a miniature Vin Diesel. The way his muscles popped out effortlessly as he took his shirt off, had me sitting there licking my lips just waiting on him to have his way with me. That V-cut of his was so sexy, and it made me want to kiss all over his entire body. As a matter of fact, I did just that. His body became a magnet to my lips as I kissed from his ear lobes until I reached his pole. You would have thought he was the size of a Vienna sausage the way I took all of him in with ease.

It took everything in me not to call on the Lord when he started twirling his tongue in my asshole; he had a bitch going nuts. For some reason, he paid close attention to my booty. From smacking, licking, kissing, rubbing, it was just a lot of ass attention. He would never let me ride him; he only wanted to hit it from the back. Which I'm ok with but damn, I wanted to show off my skills too. Now what threw me for a loop, is when this nigga asked me to suck his dick from the back. He must have lost all his damn mind when he asked that shit. I refused to do that, so then he asked to fuck me in the ass. Now that, I welcomed cause once you get it in, that shit is LIFE!

"You gone lay there and stare at me or get up and get dressed. Cookie should be headed to a meeting in a little while so if you wanted to make a move on her, now is your chance."

"If you hadn't fucked the shit out of me, yea I would have been happy to jump up like you did and get dressed."

"Aww, I'm sorry for hurting that pussy. Let me kiss it to make you feel better." He opened my legs up and started licking me how a cat lick its kittens to clean them off— all long, wide and rough.

"Umm, you know what, maybe I can just go ahead and get in the shower." I pushed him from between my legs and jumped in the shower. This nigga eats ass way better than he eats pussy, I could not lay there and even pretend that shit felt good.

"Let yourself out, I will catch up with you later," I announced as I stepped into the shower.

I wanted to get all of this man sweat off me. I'm all for good sex, but when that sweat starts dripping on my face, that's when that shit starts getting disgusting to me.

Getting out of the shower, I see this man still sitting on my bed rubbing his dick.

"Umm, don't you have somewhere to be?"

"Yea, back inside you." I had to laugh on the inside when he said that shit.

Turning my back to him, I grabbed something to put on. He stood up behind me and started nibbling on my neck. Trying my best to play hard to get, I continued to fumble through my panty drawer. I think he got tired of me playing with him because he turned me around, and put me on top of my dresser.

"What are you doing? I have stuff to… Aaahhh shit!"

Before I could finish my sentence, he already wrapped his tongue around my clit. As bad as I wanted to push him away, I couldn't, the shit was feeling too good. I'm not sure who taught this nigga how to eat pussy while I was in the shower, but I thank you.

"You taste so good," he mumbled in between sucking on my clit and twirling his tongue up and down my slit. The more he sucked on me, the harder I tried to hold back my nut. I wasn't ready for him to stop just yet. "Cum for daddy, hmm. Don't be shy baby, let me see that pussy cream."

He pulled me closer to him and started eating me like he was trying to win an Olympic gold medal. Before I knew it, I was cumming, and my juices were flowing all down his chin. He stood up, wiped his mouth, and before he walked out the door he winked at me. "See you tonight."

# Chapter 4

## Latoya "Toys" Williams

It took me a little minute to call Cookie, and when I did, she was out of town for her mother's funeral. She called me when she got back in, and I was excited as hell to meet her again. She got 500 grand on her head, and I plan on being the one to deliver. I was contacted by an outside source, and he wanted to make sure she died a slow and painful death.

I asked if he wanted me to wait until she delivered her kid since I noticed she was pregnant that night I magically came in like a shero and saved her at the club. I had my eyes on her the entire night. Once I saw she was headed back to her section, I started letting off rounds in the air. When she dove under the table, I ran over and saved the day.

Today we have plans to meet up for lunch. I figured I would weasel my way in and get her to want me even more than she already does.

"Would you like to wait a little while longer for your guest?" the waitress asked as she walked up to the table.

"Yes please, she's actually walking up right now," I announced as I saw Cookie come through the doors to the outside of the restaurant where I was waiting.

"I'm glad you asked me to meet you, these damn boys I'm carrying have my ass hungry every five minutes." She laughed, and I instantly wanted to go ahead and get the job over with.

To be so cute she's got this loud country laugh like she from the deep south or some shit. Too bad we were in public and killing her while we are sitting outside of a restaurant would not be a good look at all. For now, I will let her lil' cute country ass live.

"Not a problem, I wanted to meet you again, and I needed to get a few drinks in my system anyway. My boss has me running all over the city looking for a bitch."

"What exactly is it that you do?"

"I'm a paid contractor if you know what I mean."

"Hell yea! I need you for real. I knew it was something about you that I liked," she blurted, in an extra excited tone like her ass wanted to hire me.

"When I made it into the city the other day, on our way home someone tried to kill us. We didn't see anyone, but I know since they didn't get us the first time they will definitely try again. My fiancé said he would handle it, but now that I know you, I want to take matters into my own hands."

"Just let me know what you need me to do, and I got you. Once we are in a different location, we can discuss my fee. Even though I'm a female, just know I'm the highest paid contract killer there is." At this time the other people that were sitting outside with us have left so we can talk a little freely now. "There is not one job I have been giving that I could not complete."

I tried to assure her that I was perfect for the job. It's gone be real fucked up when the guy that hired me to kill her finds out I'm actually working for her now. Hey, I don't turn down shit but my collar, so If her money is right, then fuck him. I'ma rock with her ass. I always follow the money.

"I have to meet up with the girls in a few, but I will keep in touch with you. I'm hoping we can get this squared away quick."

"It's a done deal on my end ma, just holla at me when you ready to get started." She got up and wobbled away from the table.

I pulled out my iPhone 7 and called up the guy that put that 500 grand on her head. Maybe If I tell him she wants me to work for her and she's paying more money than he is, he just might up his pay. Again, I'm just here for the money, so I could give a fuck which one of them I kill. Fuck around, and I will take the money from them both and kill 'em after.

"We have an issue. Someone has offered me a little bit more money than you to work for them. Now unless you can top 800K, then you're on your own with getting back at Cookie," I said through the receiver.

"Bitch, who the fuck do you think you're talking to? Huh! What type of contract killer are you? I ain't never heard of this shit. If you agree to work with someone you don't quit until the job is done. Now what I can do is hire someone to kill yo ass, since you think you are so fucking untouchable."

This nigga is funny as shit. I have been following Cookie for a little while now and the man that is always with her does not look like bitch nigga.

I would snitch on his ass so fast he would really find out why the caged bird sings. What you won't do is threaten me.

"You got life all the way fucked up. Just because I'm a bitch don't mean you pump fear in my heart. We're gone end this conversation here, and I'ma let you do you. But if I find out you put a price on my head it's gone be some niggas coming after yo bitch ass. How you talking all this shit, but you hired me to get the job done for you? Cause you pussy, that's how. One thing I hate is a sweet pussy ass fraudulent ass man. Get the fuck off my line." I quickly ended the call after that.

Brandon got me fucked up if he thinks he just gone boss up on me like that. He never did tell me why he wanted Cookie dead, but I think it's time for me to let her know who is really after her.

*RING... RING!*

Pulling my phone from my purse, I saw my son picture flash across my screen.

"Hey little man, why aren't you in bed yet?"

"Because I miss you, Mommy. Mommy, is soon here yet?" he asked, leaving me puzzled.

"What do you mean, Tre?"

"I mean Mommy, is soon here yet because you promised I could come stay with you soon. So is soon here yet?" I had to hold in my laugh. He is funny asking if soon is here yet.

"It is almost here Tre, and when it comes, I promise we are going to have so much fun together. We are going to the beach, shopping, to the arcade, go carts, anything your sweet heart desires."

"Yaaaay! I'm going to pack now bye."

*CLICK!*

He was so excited that he forgot to say I love you. Tre is three years old, and he is so smart. Of course, he got that smart gene from his mother and not his father.

Pulling back up to my house, I've got out to start getting my plan together.

# Chapter 5

## Sammie "Swamp" August

My sister has me fucked up if she thinks I'm about to let her blackmail me into doing her damn dirty work. To be honest, hell mama already know I was wearing her thongs because she caught my ass one day dancing around in the mirror. After that, she used to go to the store for me every time Victoria Secret had a semi-annual sale.

Oh, let me introduce myself. You already know I am Charmaine's little brother Sammy August. I'm 22 years old, mixed with Puerto Rican and black. My hair is touching my ass; I love to wear it curly. Surprisingly, it makes the nigga's and the bitches go crazy. I got the name Swamp from this guy I used to fuck with. He said my asshole was deeper than a Swamp, so after that when I introduced myself I told them my name was Swamp and it just kinda stuck.

I am bisexual; I love the sweetness of pussy, but I love the pain of dick if that makes sense. I had my first experience with my best friend when we were in 10th grade. His mom went on a business trip, and she wanted him to stay with us while she was gone; of course, my mom said yes.

We were flipping through channels and some kind of way we ended up watching *Broke Back Mountain*. I could look at him and tell he was getting a little aroused and so was I. One thing lead to another and before I knew it his tongue was in my ass, and I was sucking his dick from the back. Just like I am about to do right now to my baby walking up to my car.

"Hey, big daddy, what you up to?" I asked Major as he walked by my car.

I love it when he plays hard to get with me. Major's been on my dick, LITERALLY, for over a year now and he still likes to play this lil' game in public. He just does not know I would expose his cock strong gay ass. For him to be so damn big, you would think he was the one who wants to give the dick. But no this nigga is on all fours every chance he gets.

"Fuck you then bitch, I'ma see that ass, later on tonight." I threw my fruit punch at his soft ass and drove off.

50

I don't understand how his ass lays with me every night and still get up the next morning and act like he does not know who the fuck I am in public. I don't know about Major, but I am not going to keep him a secret for much longer. Matter of fact, I'm going to bring him as my date to my sister's birthday party. He would have no choice but to show the real him then.

***

Driving up to my guy Turk's house, I saw him outside talking to this lil' fine ass shorty. She was fine but not for me; she was a bit Amazonish; the girl that was with her was most definitely my type though. Her ass looked like a sexy chocolate African princess— and super thick, might I add. She was rocking some tight ass pants with a cut at the knee, that looked like they were made especially for her body, small in the waist and just enough room for all that ass. Lil' mama was blessed for real. They were so tight it literally looked like Picasso sat his ass down and painted them on for her. I really could not get an up close look at her, but from a distance, she was bad as hell. I stayed in my car until they left since my boy always say I'm a lil' pretty boy and be taking all

51

his women, I kept my distance this time. But I hope and pray I run into my lil' chocolate drop again.

"What's good G, I ain't seen yo pretty boy ass in a few weeks." He dabbed me up.

"I've just been chilling trying to get my shit together, who was shorty that just pulled off?"

"Ahh shit! Look at you, that was just Krystal's lil' freak ass.

"And her friend?"

"Why? It ain't like yo ass really checking for her," he joked. "She was fine as hell though. That was my first time seeing her, so I do not have the slightest idea who she is."

Turk knows that I am bisexual, so of course he gone say some slick shit like that. If I met the right lil' baby, I would be strictly pussy— especially if the pussy was coming from my lil' African princess I just saw.

"Fuck you, how bout that!" I'ma see her again, you better believe that. What you on anyway?"

52

"Shit, about to go slid to the beach, you riding?"

"You know I keep swimming shorts in my trunk at all times." Stepping out of the car to get my clothes out the trunk. I noticed Turk looking at me sideways and started shaking his head.

"Sammie, please make sure they are swimming trunks and not no damn speedos. You know yo faggot ass will pull out some panties in a minute."

"Speaking of panties, I gotta pair of yo mama's on my back seat. She forgot 'em when I was fucking her ass last night," I quickly replied and all that damn hee hee ha ha shit stopped real quick.

"Don't play, you know I'm sensitive about my mama." He turned and walked inside the house.

Pussy boy wanna talk all that shit, but when you mention fucking his mom's he wanna turn into a bitch. I walked in the house and used the bathroom downstairs to change my clothes.

*BAM! BAM! BAM!*

"Hurry up, ion know about you, but I'm trying to find me a willing body at this beach."

Rubbing my hand over my face, and shaking my head. *This nigga,* I said to myself and opened the bathroom door.

"What you mean a willing body?"

"Nigggga, a body that's willing to let me do what I wanna do to it. The fuck! Don't worry, if I find one I'll be sure to ask if she got a brother for you, a daddy, fuck maybe even a grandpa."

"Turk, you keep on with them fucking gay jokes, I'ma end up knocking yo ass out for real. You must be mad cause I still can pull any of your bitches. Fuck outta here!" I brushed past him and went to my car.

Turk on that bullshit, I hate when people try to judge me. I am who I am, and I like what I like. But as my homeboy, once he said he accepts who I am, then why constantly joke about the shit? Like I said before, If I find a woman I wanted to be with, then I will be with her and would not touch a man or even look at one again.

"You ready?" He walked outside, and we got into his Jeep and headed to the beach. "You over there looking out the window like you got an attitude or some shit."

"Turk, yo ass be begging for me to knock yo ass out for real. I cannot help that I find men and women attractive. You find me a good female then I will be with her until then, as long as I ain't trying to fuck you then cool it on the jokes for real."

He threw one of his hands up surrender style. "Aight aight I got you. We're cool for real, my bad. I'ma find you a woman though. Matter of fact, I will call Krystal and let her know my guy wanted to holla at her girl."

"Now that's what I'm talking about, get off that dumb shit and hook me up."

We pulled up to the beach and saw all types of half naked ass females, but for some reason, I could not stop thinking about the one I just saw. Regardless if Turk helps me get her or not, I will get her one way or another; she was too damn sexy.

I took a seat in one of the chairs that were on the beach and just watched Turk throw himself at every chick with a coochie.

"Nigga, you better get out here and get some of this drunk pussy."

"I'm good bruh; you got it." He started shaking his head, and I knew the bullshit was coming, especially since he was drinking now.

"I knew yo lil' bitch ass wasn't gone do shit What did you even come here for if you wasn't gone try to fuck sum? Oh let me guess, you're waiting on the right man to come running down the beach like he on *Baywatch*."

I was so heated when he said that bullshit I jumped up and knocked his ass out. Continuously punching him over and over again until I felt someone throw me off him. He jumped up holding his lip trying to stop the blood from gushing out of it.

"I'm tired of yo shit Turk, every fucking day here you come trying to judge me. You don't think I get enough of that from the outside world and for my best friend to keep saying that shit is another smack in the face. Fuck you!" I spat, grabbing my things and walking off.

"That's right nigga walk yo ass home!" he yelled out.

"You better be quiet before he turns around and beat yo ass again." I heard a voice say that made me laugh.

Nigga, talk all that shit but couldn't hold up for any of it. I don't see what the issue is. You can't help who you have an attraction to. My mother accepted me for me, but my sister still has a problem because she is like Turk, make jokes all day long. That shit irks the fuck out of me. Fuck family and fuck friends, if they can't accept me for me.

# Chapter 6

## Tank

I still haven't spoken to Chase about that night. We have been avoiding the fact that I was coming to light his ass up that night I shot British. This shit has really been bothering me though. How could he be into some shit like that and I not know about it? I killed over 250 people for this anonymous person, and it turns out it's my brother.

The bad part about it is, this nigga is still sending jobs my way. Here I am on a plane headed to Arizona where Lexi is waiting for me. One thing that ain't stop coming since he knows it's me is the money. What he was paying me before he added 100K to each job now, I think that's worth me lying to B like I put my guns away. I just wish he didn't send Lexi ass cause that lil' fine muthafucka can definitely get it. If I wasn't scared B would beat my ass, I would have her lil' ass bent over the dude dead body after I kill his ass.

Pulling up to my hotel room where I will be till tomorrow, I had Lexi staying in the adjoining room with my next hit. I plan on making this happen quick and smooth. I need to get back home to B before her ass starts thinking I'm fucking off.

*ME: Where he at, shorty?*

*LEXI: In the bathroom. I'm about to unlock the door to the joining room. Come in exactly 10 minutes. I will make sure he is in bed.*

## ME: Gotcha!

I sent a quick text to Lex, to make sure everything was in play. Usually, I wait till it's night time to handle my business but shit It's late September, and the sun is still bussing. You know it's hot as hell when you got sweat above your top lip; I was ready to get this shit over with.

I put my bags down in my room and grabbed my tools. Once I heard the door unlock, I waited exactly 10 minutes before I crept in quietly. Lexi was riding his dick so good that nigga didn't even hear me come in the room.

"You like that, daddy?" she moaned out as she started bouncing her ass up and down on him. I felt my damn dick getting hard when I looked at her. Even with that big ass belly of hers poking out she still was a bad ass bitch.

Shit, let me get this shit over with before I get myself into trouble. She was riding this nigga like a untamed animal. I swear I heard that nigga toes popping. I wanted to laugh, but I had to get this shit over with. Once I saw him close his eyes getting ready to nut, I placed my gun to his temple.

59

"Hope they got pussy in hell, cause you won't get this last nut."

*POW!*

"Get yo shit and come into my room. Whip down everything you touched and get the fuck out. Leave this shit for the maid to clean up." She got off him and started getting her clothes back on and cleaned everything up including her juices off him. We don't need to leave no trace of her in this room.

"And wipe his mouth, cause I know you had the nigga to eat yo pussy!" I yelled back into the room.

"Shut up... I already did that, asshole." She laughed, and I watched as she went over and poured acid down his mouth and over his face.

She got everything cleaned up, came back into my room, and locked the joining door back.

"Do you mind if I shower?" I wanted to say hell yea I mind, but I knew she needed to get dude shit off her.

"Yea go ahead. I'm about to take a quick nap and get up later and grab something to eat." She went into the shower, and I laid across the bed and dozed off.

*"Shit B, I missed you so much" I could feel her lips wrap around my dick. Her mouth was always extra wet for daddy. I watched as she took in all of me with nothing but lust in her eyes. As soon as I walked through the doors, she was taking my pants off.*

*"You been gone too long, big daddy," she whispered in between sucking my dick and licking my balls.*

*I couldn't do anything but stand there and let her finish. I grabbed her by the head and started fucking her face. Holding her head down on my dick to make her gag to get my dick extra wet.*

"Wake up!" I heard someone whisper in my ear and straddle my body.

"Man Lex go head on with that shit. You know I got a woman. I came here for work and work only." Pushing her off me, she fell to the floor.

I didn't give a damn about her being pregnant; I just wanted her ass far away from me. "You already know if B found out about this she would fuck you up."

"Fuck B!" she spat, getting up off the floor, standing there asshole naked. "You know you want this good ass pregnant pussy."

"Nah bitch, I want you!" B's ass came into the room with a duffle bag and Vaseline on her face.

I wanted to laugh cause she came in like Gina when she caught Martin with Ms. Trinidad at the school. Lexi ran to the bathroom and tried to lock the door. British went over there and shot the hinges.

"The only pregnant pussy he gone be getting is mine, bitch!" She put two bullets in Lexi's head and one in her stomach. I guess her crazy ass wanted to make sure the baby was gone too.

I was standing there just looking at her because I had never been ready to fuck her ass, more than I want to right now.

"Have someone come clean this shit up and meet me in room 315," she requested and walked out the door.

I grabbed my phone and called up Chase.

"Say bruh we got a cleanup crew in Arizona?"

"Maaan, yea I thought you were leaving dude there for the maid to clean up. You must have changed plans?"

"See what had happened was, I did that job with no problem, but then yo sister-in-law wanna pop her G.I Jane ass up here, and she killed Lexi."

I pulled the phone from my ear to make sure It was this nigga on the other end of the phone laughing.

"You fucked her, huh?"

"Bruh, trust me, as bad as I wanted to, I didn't. I told her ass if B knew about this she would fuck her up and soon as I said that, B ass came in the room with a duffle bag and Vaseline. Talking about 'nah bitch, I want you'."

"Sis watches too much TV!" Chase bellowed out with laughter. He must have put the phone on speaker cause I heard Cookie ass in the background laughing too.

"That's the same thing I said. Anyway, since someone is coming to get her ass up, they may as well get dude next door too."

"I got you bruh; I will send someone there now. Go pay the front office cause I know British's crazy ass fucked some shit up." He laughed and hung up the phone.

I grabbed my shit, went to the front desk and paid the woman for the hinges blown off the door and for her troubles. I know B ass had to pay her already cause she used a key to get in. Either she paid her or pulled the gun on her ass one. Either way, she was gone get in that room one way or another.

Walking up to the elevator, I had to mentally prepare myself for the bullshit I was about to hear from B. I knocked on the door and she opened it with absolutely nothing on. My dick shot up like a rocket as I entered the room. She had rose petals and candles everywhere. It almost made me feel like I was the bitch and she was trying to get my pussy.

"So you followed me all the way to Arizona cause you wanted some dick?"

"Nah, I wanted to beat yo ass, but when I heard you tell her ass no and that I was gone fuck her up, that shit turned me on. Lexi is, well was, a pretty bitch, any man would have jumped on her ass. But you didn't." She pulled me close to her and started kissing on my neck. "You already know what you got at home is a real one and can't no one ever take my place."

I laid her back on the bed and grabbed the bottle of whipped cream that was lying next to some strawberries. Opening her legs up I sprayed it all over her pussy. I'm about to turn her ass into a sundae and I'ma put the nut on top.

***

Landing back in Miami, we both jumped into our cars that were parked at the airport and headed to a restaurant to grab something to eat. As we waited, I couldn't help but stare at British. She may do some crazy shit at times, but that's just how she shows her love for me. She must have caught me looking at her because she started staring back at me. The only difference is her eyes looked like they held back pain. I never wanted to see that look in her eyes, especially if I am the cause of it.

"Tank, why couldn't you just tell me you had to take a job out of town. You already know how my mind is and if I feel even an ounce of a bad vibe, then I will follow yo ass. I can't help it; I want you all to myself. Yo ass practically killed me on two occasions, so I don't want you to think for one second you will be able to get rid of me." She was looking at me with stern eyes making sure I understood everything she was saying to me.

"No one is trying to get rid of you, baby. I just want you to learn how to trust me. For once I want you to forget about what you been through in the past. I am not that nigga or those niggas. I am Tremaine Williams; I promise never to hurt you, neglect you, or cheat on you. I know the way we started off was rocky, I mean I practically kidnapped the pussy. What can I say? That shit was fire. I do regret not telling you about my PTSD though. A lot of things could have been avoided if I were upfront about that. It's just I had a few women I used to date, that felt like I was crazy and they couldn't handle me anymore. I did not want you to be another one that turned her back on me. I love you B, with everything in me, I want you to know that."

I reached over the table and interlocked her fingers with mine before bringing it to my mouth for a kiss. " I love you British Lynne soon to be Williams."

"I love you, Tremaine O'Ryan Williams."

# Chapter 7

## Chase

It has been forever since I had some time to myself with Cookie. For the past few weeks, things have been all over the place. From her having to up and leave to see her mom before she passed; to her having to get back home to check on her cousin. She has not had a chance to sit down and do something for herself once. So today I want to make her feel like when we first met. She told me how she felt like I was her air and I know lately it probably seems like it has been sucked out of her. She needs me to put that air in her again so she can breathe with ease. I don't want her stressing over me, British, her dad, and for damn sure does not need to be stressing over no fucking Brandon. I went out and bought all these different types of oils and flowers, and I prepared a succulent Lobster meal for us that I am sure she will enjoy.

Throwing rose petals around the room and lighting candles is only the half of what I had planned for Cookie. I hired someone to come in and give us a couples massage, and I made sure she got a little more attention because she's pregnant. I want to make sure my shorties are stress-free as well. She has been complaining about her back for the longest. At first, I thought she was just looking for attention. Mostly because it was two days after she found out she was pregnant then all of a sudden she started having cravings for pickles with a pepper mint stick, oh and her favorite hot Cheetos with cheese all over them. I don't know where she got that shit from but it sounded like the nastiest shit ever— that was until she gave me some. I damn near sucked the bag when it was empty. That shit was so damn good.

"Loooondon!" I called out to her once I finished getting the room ready.

"Yes, babe?" she walked into the room with a surprised look on her face. "What is all this, babe? You know you don't have to wine and dine me anymore, you already got the panties a long time ago."

"I would never do any of this to get something that's already mine. I just wanted to make you feel amazing. I wanted to show you how much I love and appreciate everything you do.

From taking on the girls to dealing with my crazy ass brother antics. Just seeing you smile again is the main reason for this all."

I removed her slippers and started putting edible oils on her as I started rubbing on her feet, sucking on every toe. Watching as she squirmed around on the bed, with her head thrown back, I continued to kiss up her legs until I made it to her inner thighs. For some reason, that spot was extra sensitive to her. One kiss here, two kisses there, I worked my way up until I reached her honey hole. Once my lips touched her lips, she let out a deep sign like she had been holding her breath with anticipation. I made sure I paid extra attention to her clit. When she started running away from me, I knew I was in the right spot. Wrapping her legs around my neck, I began whispering sweet words to her.

"Tell me this pussy is mine, Cook," I mumbled into her pussy. The vibration from my deep voice made her go crazy even more.

"Yes baby, it's all yours…hmmm. I promise it's all yours baby.. fuuuuckkk!" she moaned out.

I could feel her legs tightening up around my neck indicating she was about to cum. She kept trying to close her legs because she could not handle it. That shit only made me want her even more. Forcing her legs back open, I began sucking her clit so gently, making her buss all over my beard. I dragged my tongue slowly in circles around her stomach until I made it up to her neck and started nibbling on her earlobe.

"Chase, please, please stop teasing me," she exhaled, getting frustrated as I moved my dick around the folds of her lips. I wasn't thinking about that shit she was talking I wanted to take my time in this pussy.

"Fuck it!" she blurted out and pushed me off her.

I thought she was about to get up, but she straddled me and started riding me like her ass wasn't pregnant. Her pussy was gripping my dick so tight that it damn near made me nut. I didn't like her ass handling me like I was a lil' bitch. Rolling her back over I flipped her ass with one hand and gave her the dick she was begging for. She wanted me to go hard, and I did just that.

"Arch that back!" I yelled, pushing her back in. "You was begging for this dick now you wanna run from it."

*SMACK!*

I smacked her across the ass leaving my print there.

"Baby shit, wait, wait!" she moaned, throwing one of her hands back trying to push me out of her some. I smacked her hand back and made her take all of me. "Chaaase, shiiiit baby I'm about to cum!"

She tried to push me back again, but this time I grabbed both of her hands and held them back behind her like she was under arrest and I was definitely getting ready to read her, her rights. After a few good strokes, I released my seeds inside of her and at the same time she came on my dick.

She rolled on her side, put the pillow between her legs, and before I got into the shower she was already knocked out.

\*\*\*

I decided to meet Tank out for a beer. Since the girls have been here, we haven't really just kicked it without them being under us. He has been so wrapped up into keeping British ass in one place without following him, and I've been wrapped up in making sure Cookie's ass does not run off on me again.

"What's good?" Tank spoke, taking a seat at the bar.

"Shit just needed to get out that house for a little while. Between Cookie and the girls, my ass needed a break. She wants me to rub her feet, tie her shoes, lotion her legs; she's lucky she's carrying my lil' men or her ass would be doing that shit herself." He laughed, but I was dead ass serious.

"You know they say, happy wife, happy life. I swear that damn B is a loose cannon. I thought I was bad, but she is worse than I am. I found out her ass got my phone tracked a nigga can't do shit without her popping up. All I do is work though, but shorty stays thinking I'm fucking off. I had to sit her down and let her know that I don't want no other crazy bitch, just her. I've learned to deal with her crazy, so I don't have time to learn someone else's."

We were interrupted by the bartender coming up to us. "What you drinking handsome?"

"You, if you let me," Tank replied, causing me to shake my head at his ass. He was just talking about how he loves B, and don't want to deal with anyone else crazy, but here he goes with this bullshit.

"Is that, right?"

"Yea, but until then, I will take Hennessy and Coke. Oh and your number on a napkin." She started smiling at him so hard.

"I can make that happen for you," she stated then quickly turned away.

"I guess I didn't want anything to drink, huh! Her ass just said fuck me." She came back with two drinks both Hennessy and coke.

"Here this one is for you." She winked her eye at me but shit Cookie ass crazy too, I ain't about to play this game with this woman. Spinning around on her heels, she moved on to the next person.

"I hope her ass know I ain't paying for this shit. Bitch gone bring me what she wants me to have. I appreciate the free drink though."

Tank lifted his drink off the napkin, and her number was written right there. He smiled at her, threw his drink back and ordered another one. That went on until I told his ass he had enough. When Tank drinks he can turn into a totally different person. He already has issues and liquor only make that shit worse.

"Come on; I'm taking yo drunk ass home. We will get your car tomorrow."

"Can I have the check?" he asked in a slurred tone.

"Don't worry sweetie; everything was on the house. You just make sure you use that number."

He grabbed the napkin, and we both got up from the table. Before he could get outside all the way, he threw the napkin in the trash.

"Yo ass is crazy! I thought you were gonna be crazy enough to call her."

"Hell no, my nigga I just flash these hoes my sexy ass smile and get free drinks. My bitch is at home, and trust me she probably can sense when another number has been added to my phone. I ain't playing with her ass."

You can tell that nigga was dead ass serious too. He knows not to fuck with B. She got rid of Lexi's ass quick and the bitch that was in his house. I know he learned his lesson after all of that.

We got into the car and headed towards his house. He was knocked out before we even got into his drive way. I got out and helped him up the stairs. I started to ring the doorbell and leave his ass there, how Kid and Play did their drunk friend in *House Party*.

# Chapter 8

## Charmaine

"Hey sis, Swamp followed Cookie, and he thinks these pictures may help you be able to identify the man that was out there trying to kill them," Listening to him talk always make my damn ass itch.

"Guh, Give me the damn pictures," I requested.

He hates when I call him a lil' girl. I don't have nothing against him and his sexuality, but when I call him that, he gets the hell out my face talking like that. Reaching for the pictures, my eyes instantly got wide.

"What the fuck is really going on?" I questioned aloud. I was shocked to see one of our old clients. We always had issues with this nigga keeping his fucking hands to himself.

"Well, it's about time you did some shit right, baby sis! I love yooou," I joked, poking my lips out and reaching out my arms for a hug and a kiss.

"Fuck you, Swamp don't like yo ass." He mushed me in my face and left out of the office. Girls are always so fucking sensitive.

"Ay, Swamp!" I yelled out as I ran to the front door. "Don't forget my birthday dinner this Sunday. Feel free to bring a guest." He turned around and flipped me off, got in his Denali and blasted "Pay My Bills" by K. Michelle

He let the windows down and started singing.

*"Ima fuck you like I'm tryna pay bills, let me take off my weave don't wanna mess it up while I'm deep up in them sheets. A lot of time spent on my knees but I damn sholl ain't praying,"* he sang along before he sped off.

I shook my head and went back inside the house. I had too much shit on my mind to play with him today. I still could not believe after all Chase, and I have been through he just let her come in and take over shit. I lost sleep chasing behind these girls trying to make sure they were good and his business stayed afloat, and all it took was for him to meet one bitch to forget about me.

For some reason he forgets that I handled everything in his office, I know about the shit his dad has him doing. Even from his grave, he still had them wrapped around his finger.

Chase has always been a daddy's boy, anything that man asked for he would be there at his beck and call. Not that damn Tank though, that lil' nigga gave no fucks about his dad like that. I'm not sure if he mistreated him, but for some reason whenever Mr. Williams would come to the warehouse to check on things before he passed, Tank would walk past him like he wasn't standing there.

If I really, really, wanted to, I could easily take those names to the police station and have their asses in jail. But, what type of woman would I be? He would never forgive me for that, and that would surely fuck up my opportunity of making him my man. Oh well until I figure out what I am going to do about him, I will see if I can bump into this guy who tried to kill their asses.

*** 

"Hmm, shit! That feels so good, baby," I moaned out in pleasure as Major planted wet kisses all over my inner thighs.

Turning me over on my stomach, he started kissing me from my neck down to my ass cheeks. Grabbing them both, he spread my cheeks apart like he was pulling back curtains and started licking me from the Roota to the Toota. His tongue felt like it had been dipped in gold and he was trying to bury it inside of me. Not able to control myself, I started squirting uncontrollably. He sat up and watched me until I stopped shaking with a smile on his face and started back feasting.

"Stop teasing me, you already know what I want," I whispered in his ear. With that, he grabbed a magnum and slipped his dick right inside. It was different from the other time we had sex, this time it was slow and sensual. Like he knew what he came here for, and he wasn't leaving until he hit every spot and drained me dry.

"Is this what you want?" he questioned, plunging himself deeper and deeper inside of me. Caressing my breasts and kissing my neck at the same time, he had my kitty leaking and begging for him to keep going.

"This pussy so good baby, you gone have a nigga sprung."

Biting his bottom lip and wrapping his arms around my body, he rolled me on top of him. I was shocked because he refused to let me ride him the last time so I know I was about to show out. After bouncing on his dick a few good times, he grabbed my waist and held me down making sure I wouldn't move, while his dick started to erupt in the condom.

"Damn, yo ass tapped out quick."

"Shit, that's why I didn't want yo ass to ride me. Yo ass is too fat, and I already knew I wouldn't last long. That pussy was gripping my dick, and I couldn't control that shit."

Easing up off him, I went and got into the shower and sure enough the doors opened behind me and there was Major standing there in all of his glory, looking like he was ready for another round.

# Chapter 9

## Toys

"Damn girl!" Dane moaned out as I continued to ride him backwards.

He always loved that shit. Especially, when he is high as hell off a pill he just popped, and it takes longer for that nut to come. I simply turn my big ass around, grab his ankles and grind on him real slow. He likes to grip my waist and bounce my ass up and down on his dick.

Dane has always been in my corner, but I live this crazy lifestyle and being committed to him is hard to do. So I just fuck the shit out of him from time to time. I remember the first time I sucked his dick. That was the first time I let him or anyone nut in my mouth. I was trying to be a pro at that shit, so when he said he was about to nut, I kept sucking until that shit hit that back of my throat.

Maaaan, that shit scared the shit out of me. I ran to the bathroom so damn fast and spit the little nut that did get in my mouth, out. I must have coughed for 30 minutes, and he thought that shit was so funny. Talking about, 'I told you I was about to cum'.

"Babe, what yo ass over there thinking about. You made me nut then rolled over on the pillow and just started smiling at the ceiling," he asked, pulling me from my daydream.

"Just sitting over here thinking about that bomb ass dick I just got and how much I miss you. I hate I moved from Chicago and left you there. I regret that shit every day. Even though I like the money I make in my line of work, all this money does not mean shit if you are not happy."

"Toy, don't do this, you always suck me in with the tears, knowing you not gone do anything but keep fucking me and nothing more. I told you I am always here, but I won't wait forever. I'm a good dude Toya, and I'm ready for a family. You can't give me that, so maybe it's best we just cut all of this off."

He's got life totally fucked up if he thinks I'm about to just let him take my dick and run back to Chicago.

"Nope, I'm not ready to let go just yet."

I slipped under the covers and started massaging his dick with tongue. He was talking crazy, but I knew of a few ways I could change his mind.

*** 

I headed out the house to this location to meet Cookie and Chase. I'm sure they would want to hear the good news I have about who is after them. Since he didn't want to pay me more money and had the nerve to say he would hire someone to kill me. I think it's time I let them in on his little plan.

Grabbing my keys off my kitchen counter, I jumped in my spanking brand new 2017 Mustang GT Premium Fastback and did the dash to the meet up spot. I blasted "Everybody" by Kashdolls on the ride there. I looked into my review mirror and saw the police behind my ass.

Slowly pulling over, I turned off the ignition and waited on him to approach the car.

"Ma'am, do you have any idea how fast you were going?"

"Apparently not fast enough, you caught my ass."

"Excuse me?"

"No, officer. I have no idea, but I am sure you are about to tell me."

"You were doing 160 in a 70. I need you to step out of the car please."

I did as he requested and made sure I stayed in few of my own dash cam. You're not about to beat me and say your body cam didn't work. I moved to the front of my car and waited as he ran my license number in.

I watched as he grabbed his radio and started talking to someone before exiting the car again.

"I'm sorry Officer Williams, you are free to go. Have a nice day." I reached for my license, got back in the car, and headed back towards my destination.

Pulling up, I saw Cookie and Chase standing outside talking. This is my first time seeing Chase, and it feels like I have seen him somewhere before. Shrugging my shoulders and giving up on the thought of trying to figure that shit out, I got out the car and started walking towards them. The closer I got to him the more it bothered me that I could not figure out for the life of me how I knew him.

"Hey boo, I'm glad you could make it. Now, what do you have for us?"

"Damn straight to business, huh. I'm good thanks for asking," I stated in a joking tone. "I guess I should start from the beginning." Taking a deep breath, trying to choose my words carefully. I know what I am about to say, neither one of them would like it. "That night I saw you at the club wasn't a coincidence. I was actually hired to find you" I paused before I said the rest. She just stood there looking and waiting on me to get to the point.

"And kill you." Her face instantly went to the resting bitch face before she said anything. "BUT, when I met with the guy again…"

"Hol' up, guy?" She started looking puzzled, and I could see Chase starting to get pissed.

"Yes, a guy hired me. He did not go into details with why he wanted to kill you, and honestly, I didn't ask. My job is to do the job not ask questions about it, as long as the money is right."

"Look I need a name, all this extra shit is for the birds. If a nigga is out to get my wife, then I need to be a whole day ahead of his ass. So come with the shit, for real!" Chase spat, as he pulled his phone out to call someone.

"I just wanted to make sure we were good before I told you his name. Yes, I had intentions to kill you, but I felt like you would be more beneficial to me in the long run than his ass would be. You wanted to hire me on the spot for saving you from some shit that I started." I paused again to see if she would say something but she didn't. "Here!"

I handed her the pictures of the guy that hired me. Her mouth dropped open, and she ran over to where Chase was now standing.

Chase snatched the picture out of her hand and stormed over to me with fire in his eyes.

"So you mean to tell me a fucking ghost is out to kill her." He wrapped his hands around my throat and Cookie pulled her gun on me before I could even reply. "SPEAK BITCH!" he yelled out, forgetting the fucking fact he was squeezing the shit out of my neck.

I started hitting his hand and trying to push my finger in his fucking eyeballs so he could let my ass go. Before I knew it, Cookie hit me over the head with her gun and knocked me out.

*** 

"Wake that ass up!" Chase yelled out as he splashed what I thought was water in my face. But when I opened my eyes all the way, he was zipping up his pants. That lil' motherfucker pissed on me.

"Chase, I swear on everything I love G, when you let me loose I'ma personally fuck you up. I can't believe yo nasty ass just pulled an 'R. Kelly' on me." I was heated.

"Yo ass ain't gone do shit but give me the information I need. Now get cho ass up and start talking," he hissed back at me.

88

Looking around trying to focus I could see they moved me to an empty dark warehouse and it was a tall, dark skinned man standing in the corner with his arms folded just watching.

"Toys, I need you to tell me everything you know about this guy. Where and when did he approach you? Was it actually him or did someone else contact you for him? What I need to know is if yo ass physically saw this man?" Cookie spat question after question at me.

"I was gonna tell y'all crazy asses all of that before you knocked my ass out. That was a bitch move, Cookie. I shouldn't tell y'all a damn thing now. Bitch, I came out here to help you out, and this is what the fuck you do. Yo sour piss ass man wanted to use me as a fucking port-o-potty. Fuck y'all! How bout dat!" I yelled out, and before I could get another word in Cookie hit my ass again.

"Let's play fair, how about you untie me, then try to hit me like that. Ion care shit about you being pregnant, I'ma knock yo ass the fuck out."

They both had life fucked up. I am far from a weak bitch

"Like I was saying before I was rudely interrupted, Once this nigga threatened my life, I knew I had to tell you what was going on. If I don't kill you, then he will get someone else to do it for him."

Pissed wasn't even the word to describe how I felt right now. I looked up just in time to see Chase place one bullet in a revolver, spin the cylinder around then placed the muzzle against my head.

"Have you ever played Russian Roulette?" Chase asked.

"No, I haven't... Look, Chase. I'm trying to tell you guys what the fuck happened. Y'all torturing the wrong one. You need to torture that nigga with the pretty ass eyes. That's the motherfucker with the issue with you."

He pulled the trigger, but nothing came out. When I heard that click, I felt pissed trickling down my leg.

"OK, OK, OK! I met him at a club. Someone told him about me, and that was our meet up spot. He gave me a picture of you and told me how much he would pay. He even gave me his contact information to find him once the job was done."

"Now see, that is all you had to say from the jump. You took us all around the mulberry bush just to get here. Give me his information and I will handle the rest," Chase stated.

"It's in my back pocket." Cookie reached in and handed the card to Chase.

She untied me and started rubbing her stomach.

"Ok, now that we have that part under control, let's go eat bitch I'm hungry, but first I need to swing by your house so you can wash yo ass, you are starting to reek of piss; put some makeup on your face too. I don't need you walking behind me like that," She announced.

"I shouldn't go nowhere wit' yo crazy ass," I blurted, I looked into the mirror as I sat down in her car. She looked at me and laughed like something was funny.

"My bad, you don't know the history Brandon and I have. Seeing his face has sparked up so much anger and hatred that it

was hard for me to control myself. That is my ex-husband, well…
technically he is still my husband. He took me through hell and
high waters, and to actually see that he is still alive... I mean he is
actually in Miami now just puzzles the shit out of me. To make a
long story short. I caught his nasty ass fucking my best friend. I put
two bullets in her and shit I don't know how many I put in his ass. I
thought for sure he was dead, I fucked up when I didn't check to
make sure he was. That was careless of me, but I bet next time I
won't miss those vital organs."

I listened to her go on and on about what all he took her
through and how her best friend must have loved her left overs
because she fucked a few of her ex-boyfriends.

I don't know about Cookie, but Noelle would have had to
catch this fade a long time ago.

"I blame you honestly, just from what you are telling me,
you made her feel like it was ok to keep doing the shit over and
over again. Hell, let me rob you and not get punished for it, I
would do the shit again too," I replied back to her, right before she

pulled into my driveway. She stayed outside while I took a quick shower.

Once I got back in the car, she started with the bullshit again. "Make sure you throw those pissy ass clothes away."

It's still taking everything in me not to hit her ass in the back of the head. She and Chase really tried me, but don't worry; I made a mental note of that shit. I'ma play nice for right now, but sooner or later, I'ma get that ass back!

# Chapter 10

## Swamp

Pulling out of my driveway in my candy apple red Lexus, I headed towards the interstate. Today is my sister Charm's birthday party, and I promised her I would be there on time. She told me to bring a guest, but Major said he was busy and couldn't make it. He left out the house early this morning. I was finally ready for everyone to meet the new man in my life.

I told him last night I was ready to be exclusive; I was tired of being his little secret. I can't even front like that shit doesn't bother me when he acts like he doesn't know who I am when we are outside of the bedroom. He loves being balls deep inside of me and even asked if I would marry him. Now, don't get me wrong, this nigga didn't get down on one knee and ask with a ring, he just asked in between deep strokes.

I bet you guys are asking why am I talking regularly now and call myself Swamp when I'm talking to Charm, right? Well, I just like fucking with her ass. My ass really doesn't go around

94

talking about myself like that. *Swamp likes dick and not little dick, Swamp like big long horse dicks, and sweet pussy too.* Folks would really think my ass is crazy as hell.

I have a surprise for my sister, no one knows I have been recording lately and I have a CD coming out. I plan to sing happy birthday to her in front of everyone. Today was supposed to be the day I let out all of my secrets. I used to love singing when I was a kid, but for some reason, I was always told I wasn't good enough by my mother. So, I stopped trying until one day I was singing while I was fucking this guy and he started telling me how much of a beautiful voice I have. From then on out I have been in the studio, trying to become the next Trey Songz, with his sexy ass.

Exiting the expressway, I stopped at the store to get myself some peppermints just in case my voice wanted to act crazy with me today. As I approached the counter to pay for my things, I looked out the glass doors, and to my surprise, I saw my big daddy pull up. I reached for my change as I tried to make my way through the crowd of people to get to the door.

I don't know why but Arab stores are always crowded to me. Before I could get out the door all the way, I saw he was in the car with a woman. My heart instantly dropped in the pit of my stomach as I looked into her face. Feeling the tears form in my eyes, I waited for them to pull off before I walked to my car. I refused to shed a tear over him, so I quickly wiped them away. I could not believe he lied to me, though.

Here I am getting ready to announce him to everyone, and he's trying to play me. I know I love pussy too, but I stopped getting pussy when I started getting dicked down by him. He made me promise not to fuck with anyone else.

I pulled into my sister's driveway and waited a little while before I got out.

*Lord, please allow me to walk in and out of this place peacefully and not in handcuffs because they called the police on my ass, Amen.*

Getting out of the car, I slowly made my way to her steps and walked up.

*KNOCK... KNOCK... KNOCK!*

"Hey son, I'm glad you could make it," my mom said as she opened the door and reached in for a hug. "Your sister's got some big ass nigga with her, but looking at his ass, I can tell it's more sugar in his tank than yours," she whispered in my ear while hugging me. Trying to play that shit off, I walked away and laughed. She just doesn't know that nigga a whole fruit cake.

"Hey Swamp, I'm glad you could make it. Mama told me you had a surprise for me, but first I want you to meet my date, Major. Major, meet my little brother Swamp," Charm spoke, pulling me by my arm to get up close to Major.

You would have thought I was Casper the not so friendly fucking ghost, the way that man was looking at me. That nigga started shaking like a punk in a meat market. His eyes were begging me not to tell her that he had my dick on his lips, just this morning.

"What's up?" I threw my head up and went into the kitchen with my mom.

We all gathered at the table for dinner, and once it was over, they brought out the cake for her. By this time, I had one too many drinks, so I was really feeling myself and heated at the fact my sister was sitting here all over my man.

Charm stood up to thank everyone for coming to her party. As she stood up, I stared at Major until he looked at me. I blew him a kiss just to fuck with his ass. He was sitting directly across from me at the table, so I slipped my shoes off and put my feet in his lap. She continued to stand up and talk about the good man that she found and how he got her so many nice things for her birthday, all the while this nigga was sitting here giving me a foot massage.

"Again, thank you all for coming."

She took her seat and leaned over to kiss him. He moved one of his hands from my foot and held her face while he kissed her back. Once they finished kissing, he quickly went back to rubbing my feet.

"Get up Sammy, even though your voice sounds a mess, sing Happy Birthday to your sister." My mom old ugly twisted wig wearing ass is always trying to talk about some body.

"Ha ha… very funny, Ma."

I stood up and cleared my throat. "This is for my big sister, I love you, and I am so glad we, I mean you, finally found love" I walked to the front of the room as they pushed the cake out beside me and started singing.

*"You say you want me, but she needs you baby tell me what am I gonna do about this fuckin' threesome love affair,*

*If my sis comes in and catches, oh my goodness, she'll be freaked, lookin' at that big ole' dick up in the air."*

I could see the fire building up inside of Major. So I decided to switch the song up.

"I'm just joking sis, for real listen...

*Secret lovers, undercover on the DL gettin' busy in the back of his Mercedes every night."*

"Ok Swamp that's enough, you wanna tell me what the fuck is going on here?" Charm spat, standing to her feet placing her hands on her hips.

"Nah, I ain't gone tell you shit, ask yo man, since he is the one who has a lot of fucking explaining to do. Go ahead Major we're waiting! Tell my sister how you had my dick on the tip of your tongue this morning."

*SMACK!*

Before I knew it, she reached across the table and smacked the fuck out of me.

"Get the fuck out!" she screamed.

"Bitch fuck you, I've been put out of better places. But, before I go, Major are you coming with me or not? I won't ask again, just know all yo shit will be bleached and on fire if you don't."

"Let me get my coat."

He jumped up from that table so fast. My dick is too good for him to let all of this go. Fuck Charm, this is my man, I invested too much, I mean entirely too much time in his ass to let it all go to waste.

I grabbed my shit and stormed out the house after I dragged my finger in the icing of her beautiful two-tier leopard print birthday cake and licked it off my finger.

"Talk to you later, Ma!" I gave her a hug on my way out.

"I knew that nigga was gay," she whispered in my ear and started laughing.

"Ha! Bye Ma!" I laughed on the way out the door. My mom is petty as shit for real. She sat there holding in her laugh the entire time I was singing.

"Nigga don't slam my damn door like that!" I yelled out to Major as he got into the car. "You thought you could have your cake and eat it too, huh."

"Ain't that what you do with cake," he replied. I wanted to back hand his big ass.

"It's cool. I got something for yo ass when we get home." I dropped my car into reverse and sped off. Major may be bigger than me, but that nigga is pure pussy. He did right getting up from that table. He moved in with me a few weeks ago cause he needed a place to stay. I let him front in public like he doesn't know me cause I understand he ain't ready to tell the world yet, but what I won't let him do is disrespect me by coming around my family with my sister and expect me to act like everything is sweet.

***

After waking up the next morning still thinking heavy about that shit Major pulled yesterday, I realized that I could do better than him. I no longer wanted to be treated like shit. He took it upon himself to go the extra mile to lie to me about why he couldn't go with me to meet my family. If he felt the need to do all that for her knowing I am the one who always opens my doors up to him then that clearly shows that he does not give a fuck about me. So from this point on it's FUCK MAJOR AND FUCK MEN PERIOD!

"Get the fuck up!" I spat, shaking him back and forth. He was laying up here like everything is cool and it's not.

"Gone on with that shit now Swamp, it's too early." He replied and pulled the covers up over his head. I see he want to play with fire huh.

102

"Major, I'm telling you to get the fuck up out my bed. I don't want to do this shit no more. That shit you pulled yesterday was the last straw for me, and I'm done." He started snoring, completely ignoring me, so I did what I had to do.

"AAAAHHHHH!" He jumped out of bed screaming once he felt the flames from the fire hit his leg.

"I said get the fuck out." Grabbing his shit, he ran out the house.

I went into my kitchen to get the fire extinguisher so that I could put the little fire out in my bed. That bitch could have burned to the ground I would not have cared as long as his ass was out of my house. I'm ready to start my new life, nothing but pussy from here on out. I promise.

## Chapter 11

## Cookie

I laid in my bed looking at the ceiling. The more I thought about all of this, the angrier I became. I was supposed to get rid of Brandon and never have to worry about him again. For some reason, Chase thinks Charmaine is behind the shooting. The way I am feeling now, I just may pay her ass a home visit.

Grabbing my phone, I called up British.

"Say lil' baby, throw something comfortable on and take a ride with me."

"Bitch you would call when I'm about to get some dick," Brit replied with a long huff.

"Bitch, by the time I get dressed and get there, trust me Tank's quick pumping ass should be done."

"'Watch ya mouf, one thing I won't let no bitch do is talk about my man. Now, I can talk about his short strokes all day."

I laughed aloud at her ass; she is a whole fool.

"Girl shut up, and hurry up. I will be there in 30 minutes." I disconnected the call and rolled out of bed.

My big ass can't fit shit no more, so I went right into Chase closet instead of mine. Pulling out a Nike t-shirt and grabbing my Nike legging out of my dresser drawer, I dropped my piece maker in my bag and headed downstairs.

Chase was already out and about so I had no one to question my whereabouts. He didn't care where I went as long as I had Major with me.

Stepping outside, I waved at Major to pull the car around. I refused to walk over to the mini car lot we have next to the house.

"Thanks, I'm headed to British house to pick her up then we have to go visit an old friend."

"Do I need to come with you?"

"Nope, I need you to stay right here."

I didn't want him having a reason to call Chase. The less he knew, the less he could tell.

I turned my Ro. James on from my iPhone 7 and cruised all the way to British's house. I was trying to get my plan together before I said something to her. But shit, from the looks of things we will just go for what we know.

"Climb out the pussy gawd dammit!" I said as I spoke through the intercom so they would open the gate for me. One thing for sure, Tank's got this bitch stashed away nicely.

"Must you be ghetto every time you come over?" British sneered, as she started walking down the steps.

"No, but ghetto is much more fun, Get in!"

"Where are we going? I have an oral contest at seven o'clock."

"An oral contest?" I said with my face twisted up. "What the hell is that?"

"Girl it's this game Tank, and I like to play. We set the alarm to see who can make the other cum the fastest. His ass has been beating me bad, so tonight is our rematch round. I'm trying to make that nigga tap out." She laughed and kicked her feet up on my dashboard. "Where we headed?" She quickly questioned, like her ass know when I ain't up to no good.

"I'm not telling you until we get there. Yo ass is gone try to talk me out of it."

"You better tell me, or I'ma call Chase on yo ass and tell him you're up to no good."

"Bitch!" I blurted looking at her with the meanest mug on my face. "I just wanted you to tag along while I paid Charmaine a visit. Chase thinks her ass was behind the driver getting shot."

I studied her face to see if she was going to tell me it was a bad idea, but she just kept looking out the window.

A little while later, we pulled up to her house. I saw her car in the driveway, so I got out and knocked on the door.

*KNOCK... KNOCK... KNOCK!*

*KNOCK... KNOCK!*

Before I could get that last knock in, she swung the door open.

"The fuck you want?" she practically screamed out at me. I immediately felt my body fill up with rage and before I knew it, I pulled my gun out and pointed it at her temple.

"If I find out you sent somebody after my family and me, I'ma come back here and blow your fucking head off," I said through clenched teeth.

"Bitch, fuck you, I ain't send nobody nowhere, I could give a fuck about y'all," she argued.

"You heard what the fuck I said, I'ma make sure I pay yo mama a visit first, then yo funny ass sister/ brother Swamp, then I'm coming for you. Please don't test me!" I spat, releasing her hair from around my hand. "Let another bullet come my way, and you're gonna have six coming at you." She was now standing there with tears in her eyes.

"Cookie, I promise I didn't shoot at you," she pleaded.

"Fuck that shit you're talking. Just know if that shit happens again, yo whole family is gone be fucked up, and you better pray ya grandmother's already dead cause bitch I'ma work my way down ya family tree till I get to yo ass."

Spinning around on my heels, I headed back to my car. British was still sitting there calm without a care in the world.

"I thought I had to call the cleanup crew on yo ass. You pulled that gun out kinda quick, sis," she said as she blew a big bubble with her gum. "Girl look at this picture, ain't it cute?" She asked showing me a picture on her phone of her and Tank.

Tank has really turned her into a monster. I didn't expect that nonchalant attitude, but I guess I forgot that she had more bodies under her belt than I do. She told me about the bitch she shot in the head. Let's not forget to add while Tank's dick was in the girl's mouth. So, I should have known that she would be with this shit from the jump.

"Let's go get food; I'm hungry," British announced, rubbing on her still flat stomach. She had the perfect body, even while pregnant. I, on the other hand, gained the freshmen 15 the second month of being pregnant.

We pulled up to Popeyes and ordered us something quick so we could get back home before the guys noticed we were gone to long and start asking questions.

"Thank you," I said to the young lady as she reached my food out to me.

Suddenly I heard tires screeching behind me, so I quickly look into my review mirror, only to see this black car coming full speed towards me.

"Oh shit!" I screamed out, trying to put my car into drive but it was too late; my car was hit from the back full force. I kept pushing on the breaks to stop myself from moving, but they pressed on the gas even harder trying to push us into traffic.

"Cookie, what the fuck is going on?" British yelled out as she grabbed her phone to call Tank. The car behind us stopped, the tires started spinning really fast, and this time we went flying into the middle of the highway.

*BOOM! BOOM!*

# Chapter 12

## Tank

"Bruh, we have to sit down soon and discuss some shit. It seems like you have been avoiding the issue, and it's some shit I really need to get off my chest," I spoke to Chase as we sat outside in the front waiting on the girls to pull back up.

"Real shit Tank, I didn't know it was you working for me, or I would have found someone else. When dad died, he left two things behind. One being, what we do with the girls and two being the list of motherfuckers who crossed him. He even left money behind to make sure the jobs were handled. Did I want to become a hit man? Hell no! That shit ain't in me unless they crossed me. I have no idea what these people did to pops, but I promised him I would get it done. His other request was me not to tell you because he knew you had PTSD and thought this would only make it worse, which it did. Shit, you wanted to kill me!" I said holding my hands up surrender style.

"In my defense, I was going to kill my boss, who just so happened to be you. British made my ass start back seeing my shrink, and that is when I discovered that hearing gun shots triggered my dreams."

"Look, just know I didn't mean any harm by not telling you what was up. I did it to protect you more than anything. You did a good ass job by the way. That's why when I found out it was you that night, I still didn't find someone else to take your place. I might as well keep giving you that bread for you and all those kids you about to keep popping in B."

"Fucking right! I need that cash, for real!" I blurted, "Hol' up; this is her calling right now."

"You better make sure you come home with food cause y'all asses been gone all day," I spoke into the receiver as soon as I answered the phone.

"BABY LISTEN, SOMEONE IS TRYING TO HURT US. WE ARE AT POPEYES ON SHELBY DRIVE, AND IT'S A BLACK CHARGER RAMMING INTO US PUSHING US INTO TRAFFIC. BABY PLEASE, GET HERE!" she screamed out to me. By this time, I had already grabbed my damn keys and pulled Chase towards the car with me.

"B, calm down I'm headed to you right now, I have Chase with me. Stay on the phone, baby, what's going on now?" I tried my best to keep her calm, but I could hear her screaming in the background every time something crashed into them. The last sound was so loud I had to pull the phone back from my ear.

"British… British… please say something!" I pleaded, but my calls went unanswered. I could hear people talking and calling 911.

"Tank, what the fuck is going on, bruh?" Chase questioned.

"Someone in a Charger is ramming into them." I can hear someone calling 911."

By this time, we are around the corner from where she said they were located. The traffic was so backed up we had to get out the truck and run up to where they were.

"Hold on sir; you can't be here." The officer tried to pull me back, but I was not about to let him stop me from getting to her.

"Get the fuck off me!" Chase pushed through the other officers and made his way to Cookie.

113

They were using the Jaws of Life to get her out of the car. The officer that was holding me moved out the way, once I knocked his ass out. Running over to the ambulance they had British in, I jumped in with her.

"Are you her husband?" the EMT asked, as soon as I sat down beside her.

"Yes and she's pregnant, so y'all motherfuckers need to do whatever the fuck you need to do to make sure they are good!" I spat as I sat there holding on to British's hand.

She had cuts on her face from the glass shattering, and they had a brace around her neck so that she would not try to move it before they checked her out. Looking at her, I could see the tears rolling down her pain-filled eyes. I wanted so badly to take her pain away from her, but most importantly, find out who in the fuck did this shit.

"Where's London?" she whispered.

"Chase is over there with her right now. You just lay back. We are headed to the hospital." She started kicking and screaming,

"LET ME OUT OF THIS MUTHAFUCKA NOW, I NEED TO CHECK ON MY COUSIN!"

"Baby, calm down, you have to make sure you are good. They are working on getting her out of the car and Chase is right there with her."

Now I see why they had her ass strapped to the bed. She was doing all she could to get out of the ambulance. I wanted to tell her Cookie was ok, but from the looks of her car and the car that ran into the side of her, things do not look too good. The driver that hit them flew out of the front window, the side Cookie was on was crushed, and when I ran passed her car, she was slumped over the wheel unconscious. Finally looking out of the back window as we pulled off, I saw them pull the stretcher to the car and place Cookie on it.

"Everything is going to be ok, B. I just need you to hold on ok! Are you gone hold on for me?" Placing a kiss on her forehead, I could feel her give my hand a squeeze. "No matter what, I want you to know that I love you, and I am so sorry for everything I have put you through."

115

"Her heart rate is dropping!" the EMT yelled out. Sitting there trying not to panic, I kept talking to her. Continuing to whisper in her ear, I started to go down memory lane with her.

"Baby, you remember that time we were at the beach, and you were sooo scared to get in because you thought it had sharks in the water. You remember that, B?" I tried so hard to hold back the tears as I watched them work on her, but one tear managed to escape. "You kept saying, babe, I watch too much TV to get into that water." I spoke trying to match her tone. "I know it's sharks in there just waiting on me.

I told you nothing was in the water, and I just wanted you to get in so I could take a picture of you with a wave behind you. Once you got in you was standing there looking good as hell, the sun was making your skin glow, and the water was splashing against your legs. When I reached down to pull my phone out of my pocket, you started yelling, 'Shark, Shark, Shark'!"

Pulling her hand close to my mouth and planting several kisses on the back of it. I was trying to fight through the tears, so she wouldn't hear my voice trembling. "You were so scared baby, and if I had not seen the human feet on this shark. I would have been scared too. When you saw it was a kid with a shark fin on his back, you tried so hard to strangle that little boy. That was the funniest shit ever. I probably didn't get the picture I wanted of you, but I got that picture for sure."

"Pulse is good, BP is 120 over 60," the EMT announced as we pulled up to the hospital.

I watched as they pulled her out first then I followed right behind her. Not caring what they said, I needed to be right beside her through all of this. I refused for her to wake up and I was not there.

I watched through the glass as they started cutting her clothes off, making sure they didn't miss any injuries. I slowly walked away. She was starting to cut up again, and I felt myself getting ready to knock out a doctor. Pacing the waiting room back and forth, I was damn near losing my mind worried about her and my babies. I took a seat in the chair next to the door. Placing my head down on my lap I started talking to the only person I know can make this alright. *British has been through enough Lord, all I ask is that you see her through this and I promise you I will lock her up in her room, so I know for sure she is safe at all times. Lord, you can call me crazy all you want, but you made me like this and you know they say we are made in your image. Just please make this okay for us, please Lord just make this okay.*

"Bruh, step out here for a second. How is British doing?" Chase asked.

"Man, I don't know, I had to leave from by the door once they started removing the glass from her face and examining her body. She had so many cuts and bruises. I don't think anything was too fucked up about her though besides that. I tried to look over her my damn self while we were in the ambulance. Her heart rate started dropping on the way here. I tried to keep her conscious. So I started talking about a trip we had to the beach. I was just thinking of anything to say to keep her calm while they worked on getting her heart rate steady. How's Cookie?"

"Honestly, I can't even say. I know for sure her leg is broken, the car crashed into her on the driver side, and the door jammed into her side. They monitored the babies the best way they could on the way here, and they seemed ok. They put her on a monitor to check them while they examined her right when we made it here. She is in surgery, so now we play the waiting game."

I could see the tears filling up in his eyes. My brother has never shown emotions like this for anyone other then Monica his wfe. I know he loves Cookie with everything in him, just like I love B. If anything happened to those girls I, for one, would lose it and everybody would have to pay.

"Fuck man! I can't believe something like this happened to them. This shit is getting out of hand. I have to find out who is doing this shit," he blurted out, rubbing his hand over his face.

"Why wasn't Major with them anyway? That's what you pay that nigga for. You need to holla at him on the real, before I do."

I walked away, punching the wall that we stood across from. Something wasn't right with that nigga, and I will most definitely find out what it is.

"You gotta calm down, or they gone put yo ass out of here," Chase stated like I really gave a fuck about them putting me out. My wife is back there in fucking pain; I could give a fuck about anything else.

# Chapter 13

## Brandon

They say only the good die young, and I'm a fucked up nigga. Ain't no good bone in my body. Cookie fucked up when she didn't make sure I was dead. Now, Noelle on the other hand, that bitch is dead, and Cookie made sure of that. She gave her straight shots to the dome.

I can't even front like she didn't fuck me up, cause she did. A nigga was down bad. I was out of it for a while until the cleanup crew came in. I recognized the voice instantly cause the lil' nigga used to blow Cookie's phone up when we first got together. When that pussy ass nigga Chase left, and it was just Justin and his crew there, once I knew he was gone for sure, I made it known that I was still alive. Here's what happened...

*"Load him up, and I will take him out while you guys finish cleaning the rest of this shit up," Justin demanded, as he moved around before pushing me out of the door. As soon as I felt the night air hit my wounds, I started gasping for air. He instantly dropped me on the ground and pulled his gun out.*

121

*"What the fuck? Are you some type of Houdini or some shit?"*

*He kept his gun aimed at me as I started to force myself to speak. One of the bullets hit me in the stomach, and it was making it hard for me to breathe.*

*"No," I said just above a whisper. "I was never dead; I continued to lay there like I was dead until I heard them leave. I recognized your voice when you came in."*

*He started looking weird in the face like I didn't know he used to be with Cookie. I wasn't going to tell him just in case he felt like he wanted to go back and tell them I was still alive.*

*I knew money would always sweeten the deal, and trust me it didn't take much money either. I started off low prepared to go higher, and he took my first offer. That nigga took them five stacks and ran. He drove me to Baptist Hospital and went to meet Chase and Cookie.*

And now I'm here, back and stronger than ever. I already knew her location once I found out she moved out of the house.

Since I used to buy pussy from a few of Chase girls, I knew that's where they went. I have been laying low here for a week or so now. I'm just waiting on the right time to show my face again.

"Thank you for meeting me on such short notice," I spoke to Charmaine as she walked up to the table, pulling me from my thoughts. I was sitting outside of a restaurant waiting on her arrival.

"It's good to see a familiar face around here for once. I see yo ass is still thick as fuck," I spoke as I pulled her in for a hug, glancing down at her booty.

"You know this ass is gone always be right if nothing else is." She took a seat at the table and ordered her a drink.

"It seems like you and I have a common interest. I was following Cookie the day you rammed your car into hers. At first, I thought it was just an accident until you kept doing it over and over again. Once you sped off after two cars hit her, I decided to follow your car to see who you were. At first, I couldn't see your face until you made it to where you ditched the car at. Now, my only question is what's your issue with her?"

123

She sipped on her drink before she started talking about how Cookie showed up and took over everything. She fired my good piece of ass, Duchess and then Charmaine.

It seems like little London Bridges done grew some hair on her pussy, and now she's smelling herself. Trying to act like this woman that I know she ain't.

Granted she took her shots on our asses for real, but she ain't bout that life. I can't wait to put that hot lead back in her ass. I sat there damn near tuning everything she was saying out, trying to think of my next move. Since that lil' bitch I hired turned snake on me, I have to figure out a new way.

"B... Brandon, are you listening to my ass? I asked you, how do you know Cookie?"

"She's my wife."

"YOUR WIFE?" Charmaine exclaimed.

"Yea we are still married, she caught me sleeping with her best friend, and she tried to kill our asses. She did get her friend though, but I survived the bullets she let off in my ass. That's why

I'm back. I wasn't trying to shoot the driver; I was aiming for Chase first. When I get to her, I want that shit to be painful. I plan to make her my last target. She tried to kill me and killed my good pussy having ass side piece, so there's no way I can let some shit like that slide."

Before I came here to meet Charmaine, I was camped out at the hospital trying to wait it out until Chase left.

"Just tell me what I need to do. That bitch said she was gone kill my entire family if I came at her again, and I don't take kindly to threats. I need to get her before she tries me. She pissed me off that day she came to my house and tried to check me. She just doesn't know if I had my gun beside the door where it usually is, I would have blown her fucking head off. I pulled the fake tears on her ass, so the bitch definitely thinks she got the upper hand and I'ma weak bitch. She's got a rude awakening coming for her ass tho!" Charmaine bellowed as she balled her fist up in anger.

"Just chill shorty… I have a plan."

Once you take out the head, the body will definitely fall, and I plan on doing just that. It seems like Chase has his head so

125

far up in Cookie's ass, all it is going to take is for his precious little jewel to be taking from him.

"Let's cut this meeting short; I will keep in contact and let you know what my next move will be."

"Please do! Where are you staying here?"

"In a hotel trying my best to lay low."

"You can always stay at my place if you are tired of spending money. I'm sure this shit will be over with before we know it," she added.

Kicking it at her spot wouldn't be a bad idea. I can figure out a plan and get some pussy at the same time. Charmaine has always been my cup of tea, she a lil' bald headed, but I can work with that. It's nothing a few bundles can't fix.

"That sounds good to me. I will check out today and meet you at your place. Make sure you send me the address and don't be bullshitting either Charm. I know how yo ass can get down sometimes," I announced, as we both got up from the table and went our separate ways.

The first thing I did was head back to the hospital waiting on the perfect time to go up and visit my wife. Sitting in my car with the Stevie J grin on my face, this is about to get real interesting.

# Chapter 14

## Cookie

"Chase… Chase…" I spoke as loud as my voice would allow since my throat was extremely sore. Looking around, all I could hear was machines beeping and buzzing continuously. A monitor was around my stomach, and my leg was propped up in a sling with a cast on it.

"Chase… Chase…" I tried calling out again. He jumped up off the chair. He was asleep in the corner.

"Hey baby, how are you feeling?" He pulled the chair up beside my bed, grabbed my hand, and stroked my hair back off my face.

"I'm ok, in pain but I will be ok. How are my babies, did you make the doctor check them?

"They are both doing just fine. The car that rammed into the side of you crushed the front fender into your leg, that's why they have it up in a sling. It is completely broken, and you will need to stay off it for a while. Do you remember anything about what happened?" I laid my head back, closed my eyes, and tried my best to remember.

"I can remember British and I leaving from Charmaine's house and going to Popeyes cause we both were hungry as hell. Once I reached for my food, we were rammed in the back. I tried my best to stop them from moving my car, but they had their foot pushed so far down on the pedal it was hard for me to stop. On top of that, whoever it was made me drop my damn food and I'm still mad behind that shit." I gotta make a note that when they find whoever this nigga is that I get my damn $5 back. Two things I will not play about are my meat and my meals.

"You remember what type of car it was?"

Chase was asking me so many questions. I know he is just trying to figure out who did this, but shit, Popeyes has a camera so go pull the damn tape. I for one do not feel like talking about it anymore.

"No, maybe British got a good look at it. If you don't have much to do today, you can always go see if Popeyes has a camera maybe they will let you look at the footage."

129

"Bet, I will do that. I love you!" He kissed me on my forehead and headed towards the door.

"Damn, I didn't mean right now!" I spat. "I know you are trying to figure this shit out, but shit Chase, I'm in pain and right now I do not want to be left alone." He slowly turned around and came right back beside me.

"I'm sorry, I wasn't thinking. I'm just trying to do my best by protecting you, but I can handle that shit later. Just know once yo ass falls asleep I will dip. Tank and I gotta handle this issue for real."

That was perfectly fine with me, but as of right now I just wanted my man beside me.

***

Waking up from a deep sleep I could feel someone standing over me. Slowly peeling my eyes opened, I reached out for Chase's hand. I saw someone standing there, and I wanted him to come closer to me not just stare at me.

"Come here baby, did you find out anything?" I questioned.

"I found out my wife is a bigger whore than I ever was. How you go and get knocked up already but couldn't carry my seeds?"

The voice I heard caused me to wake up all the way and look around the room. My eyes landed on Brandon, and I damn near shitted a brick. I started pressing down on the call button. "Don't worry, I will run into you again. But next time I will make sure you don't get away from me." He rushed out of the room as soon as the nurse came through the door.

Breathing heavily, I managed to get out that someone was just in my room. I reached for the phone, so I could call Chase and let him know Brandon was just in my room.

"Wake up, Ms. Bridges." I felt the nurse moving me from side to side. Peeling my eyes open, she and two other nurses were standing around my bed.

"You were having a dream. We heard you screaming and rushed inside. You would have thought someone was really in here killing you the way you were screaming. Are you ok?" one of the nurses asked.

"No one was just in here?" I asked.

"No ma'am, your husband made it clear before he left that no one other than your doctor or a nurse was to enter your room. He even has this big buff fine man at the door watching you. Everything is ok, sweetie."

They checked my vital sounds, listened to the babies again then left out of the room. My heart was still racing because that dream felt too real to me. I even still smell his cologne in my room. Grabbing my phone, I called up Chase and asked him to get to me as soon as possible.

I pressed the call button again so the nurse could come in. I wanted someone to take me to see my cousin. If it wasn't for me trying to do a pop up on Charmaine, she would not be in this position now. If something had happened to her, there was no way I would have been able to live with myself.

The nurse came in and helped me ease my way into the wheel chair. Luckily, she said British was right down the hall. When she pushed me into her room, I couldn't do anything but cry looking at her. She had her entire face wrapped in bondage white wraps with blood seeping through some areas. I couldn't stop the tears from falling looking at.

"Cook, don't bring yo ass in here with all that crying cause I know it ain't nobody but yo ass."

She made me laugh because her face was completely wrapped up, eyes covered and all, and she still knew it was me.

"I'm sorry, cousin. I shouldn't have asked you to come out with me. I put your life in danger and Tank's ass is gone kill me if something happens to you." I rubbed the back of her hand and tried to get as close to her bed as my leg would allow. "You got room for me up there."

"Girl yea, slide yo ass on up here." Standing up on my good leg, I eased into the bed with her and used one of her extra pillows to prop my leg up. After talking to each other trying to figure out what happened, both of our asses fell asleep.

# Chapter 15

## Toys

"Have you seen him yet?" my best friend Ronnie asked through the receiver.

"No, I saw his brother and his fiancé, but not him. Honestly, I don't even know what I will say to him once I see him again. We have been separated for so long. He probably would shit a brick if he saw me, if not try to kill my ass since I did just walk out and leave him. Not to mention while I was pregnant with his child that he did not know about."

So many things are going through my head right now. After I had come back home from being out with Cookie, I kept racking my brain trying to figure out how I knew Chase. Then it hit me that he was Tank's brother.

"I'm sure you will come up with something."

"Yea, I know. I wonder if he still looks the same. He has always been my Denzel in my head." I laughed.

It was something about him that always made my heart flutter when he walked into the room. He and I were dangerously in love and truthfully, we were bad for each other, but only because we both had a fucked up life. We were hurt by other people and never healed from that pain. Two broken people trying to be together and love each other, only caused more pain. Everything about him was perfect, but when it came down to me, he would lose it all for my happiness. In a way that was a good thing until I witness him kill someone over me. I didn't want him to throw his life away for me, so I just left one night he was sleeping.

"You're silly girl. I'm about to get ready for work. If you need me I'm only a call away, sis," Ronnie announced, pulling me from my thoughts.

"Oh yea, girl I know I can always call on you. I'm about to get out of here anyway. I have to go play nice with my sister-in-law. Maybe I can use her to help me get to him."

"Ok Toys, I love you."

"I love you too, sis!" We both clicked the phone, and I sat back on my couch just thinking of how I would make this shit happen sooner than later.

Cookie got out the hospital today, so I'm going to make it my business to go and visit her. I need her on my side and know I'm not here to start any shit. I just simply want my husband back. It crazy how this shit all came into play so perfectly. Who would have thought I would be introduced to Cookie's ex and who knew she would turn out to be with my husband's brother.

Tank and I met years ago when we were both deployed to Iraq. He was really going through it there. We kinda found peace in each other. That was until he started acting crazy after his friend was killed. Once we got back to the states, we started seeing more and more of each other and started dating. He came up with the bright idea to get married for the extra money, so we did. At first, it started off as a money thing, but then we started really falling for each other. One thing led to another and BAM I was pregnant.

I have been trying to find a way to get in close with Cookie and Chase before I introduced the real me, but I think I almost fucked shit up when I told them I was sent to kill her. Even though that shit her and Chase pulled was fucked up, I do understand why they were so quick to do what they did. I mean if I tried to kill a nigga and left his ass for dead, and he showed up out the blue, I would be ready to kill a few bitches too.

Sitting up in my bed, I pulled out an old picture of Tank and I. I just stared at it smiling while thinking of all the good times we had together. The times we had before he started using me as a punching bag when he used to have his little episodes. It took me a while to leave because I was trying to stay because I know losing me would make his PTSD even worse. It took everything in me to leave him. I must have changed my mind over a million times. Over the years, I have come to realize that I fucked up and should have stayed with him. Now, I have to find a way to get him back. Legally he is mine, but with his new bitch British, I don't know if this will be an easy process.

I walked out my room into the living room where my car keys were located, grabbed them and left out the house. It was another beautiful sunny day in Miami, so I cruised the city a little bit before heading to Cookie house.

***

"Hey sweetie," I spoke as I walked into her bedroom. She was lying there with her leg elevated and watching reruns of *Martin* laughing like she has ever seen it before.

"I came bearing gifts, and this one is for you." I passed her a big ass balloon with a teddy bear in the inside of it that read *Get Well Soon* on the t-shirt.

"This one is for British, I know she does not live here, but I'm sure someone can get it over to her for me.

"Thanks, girl." She had the biggest smile on her face. "How have you been?"

"I'm good just trying to figure out how all of this keeps happening to you guys. What type of security do you have? Cause that nigga is never in pocket. It seems like you need to hire me for more than one job cause that nigga sholl ain't doing his."

"That would be a good idea, but I don't know you like that. You just told us that you were sent here to kill Cookie, and now you are sitting here trying to be her personal security guard. If I find out you still working for that fuck boy we gone play another game of Russian Roulette— only this time a bullet will be in each chamber. Cookie doesn't need no bullshit around her right now. She needs some solid ass muthafuckas. Now either you gone be that without the bullshit, or we're gone have a few problems."

Chase appeared out of nowhere in the door way, startling me. I'm definitely not here on bullshit. If she needs me by her side 24/7, I will do that.

"You don't have to worry about me crossing you guys but what you need to worry about is why her security ain't doing his job. Either he's working for her or he's not. None of this should be able to happen to her. On top of that, she only has one bodyguard and if you ask me, he ain't much of one. It seems like he worried more about getting fucked in the ass than making sure she is safe."

"What?" Chase questioned.

"Yea, I do my digging on everybody that I end up around. I don't trust no one around me, just like you. I had a funny feeling about that nigga when he was at the warehouse in the corner watching y'all torture my ass. I followed him one day he left from there, and he went right to some bitch nigga with long ass hair. Can't no dick in the booty ass nigga protect her. You need to get some real hittas on your team, Chase. I don't even care about the money anymore I'm just here cause when I first met her we clicked. I mean granted she was just a job, but again, we clicked, and I never try to get close to someone I know I will eventually kill. I have been trained by the best. My father made sure I knew how to handle my own shit."

"Aight, you don't have to keep going. We will see how this shit works out, but I'm telling you Toy, one fuck up and we're gone cut yo ass off and cut yo ass up, simple as that. I don't usually hit females, but you look like you got a dick; so I will definitely lay yo ass out for fucking with mine."

I almost told that nigga to suck my dick when he said that shit. Don't shit about me scream man, but my hands because I will knock a muthafucka off their feet. With that, he spun around and left out the room. I turned back towards Cookie, but she was knocked out. Leaving the balloons and bears beside her bed, I made my exit.

***

Waking up the next morning, I was happy as hell because my son is coming today. I left him back home with my mother while I came here to handle business. I finally decided it was time for him to come live with me, so I found us a nice comfortable house right outside of Miami. I spent the entire morning going to buy him new toys, books, and games for us to play. He loves to read, so one side of his wall is a bookshelf filled with tons of books he loves. I can't wait to see his cute little face and most importantly introduce him to his father.

I show Tre pictures of Tremaine all the time, so he will know who he is when he finally does get to see him. I'm happy the time is coming now while he is young instead of when he gets older because then he would really resent Tank for not being around him. I just pray all of this works out in my favor.

Pulling up to the train station where he and my mom where arriving into, I already know he is going to run to me and give me the biggest hug and kiss ever. It's been three months since I held him and my heart is screaming for him.

Moments later, he and my mom stepped off the train. Once he laid eyes on me, we both ran full speed at each other with our arms held out.

"Mommy! Mommy! Mommy. I've missed your pretty face so much." I couldn't do anything but laugh at him. For him to be only three, I swear he has an old soul.

"Mommy missed my handsome man so much." Planting multiple kisses on his cheeks, we headed to the car.

"Damn, mama can't get a hug?" my mom spoke up. I forgot all about her when I saw my baby. She will be here until tomorrow then she's getting back on the train and headed home.

"Sorry Ma, I got so wrapped up into Tre. You know when he is around nothing else matters to me anymore. Not saying that you don't matter, but you understand what I'm saying." I reached in for a hug, and she kissed my forehead.

"I know what you meant sweetie; I was just joking. Take me back to the house so I can lay down. I know you guys have a big day planned."

I grabbed her hand, and we walked to the car.

# Chapter 16

## British

After being released from the hospital with only a few minor injuries, Tank and I were finally heading home. I wanted to go by Cookie's house first to check on her, but he refused. He wanted me to get in the bed to rest. Talking about he talked to God and told him if he makes everything ok for me, he would lock me up in my room and make sure nothing else happened to me. Truth be told, I believe his ass too. Any man that's capable of woman-napping you for days will have no problem with locking yo ass up. I just sat back in my seat to prepare myself for a life of boredom cause this nigga does not let up once he has his mind set on something.

"You need anything before we get home?" he asked as we pulled off from the hospital.

"I would love to have my Popeyes that I paid for before that bitch rammed into us."

"Bitch? Did you get a good look at her face?" He stopped the car in the middle of traffic and gave me a stern look.

"Somewhat babe, I just remember seeing blond hair."

He positioned the car in drive and sped off. Moments later, we pulled up at Popeyes, and he made me get out of the car. I was unsure of what he had plans to do, but shit, we could have grabbed my chicken from the window.

"Where's yo manager at?" he announced upon walking into the restaurant.

"I'm the manager on duty, how may I help you?"

He asked if we could talk in the back. At first, you could tell that she did not want to, but once he showed her the gun on his hip, she quickly pushed us to the back.

"Now, I'm not here on no bullshit. I'm not trying to rob you or nothing like that, but a few days ago my lady was in a car accident right outside of this restaurant, and I really need to see that tape from that day."

"I'm sorry sir, but those tapes are already gone. A man came in here yesterday and retrieved everything we had." Looking at Tank, I could see he was pissed off.

"Do you remember what he looked like?"

"I don't. I was not on duty when he came. I was told once I came in. I'm sorry I couldn't help you, and I really hope you find out who did this, especially if it was done deliberately." She stood up from her seat indicating it was time for us to leave.

He reached for my arm, and we walked out of the restaurant, but not before his ass walked into the kitchen and fixed me another box of spicy chicken wings with red beans and rice. We got back inside the car and headed towards the house.

***

"Wake up, babe," I said, pushing Tank from side to side.

*BUZZZ... BUZZZ!*

"Get up and see who's at the gates, Tank."

Reaching for the remote with his eyes still closed. He pressed the button, and the camera on the TV popped on. It was his mom and sister Cassie. I only knew it was them from the pictures that Tank had around the old house.

"Get up Tank; it's your mom." He jumped out of bed like he all of a sudden had a burst of energy.

"Quick, get dressed and make sure it's something decent too!" he spat. I continued to watch him rush around the room throwing on clothes. "I SAID GET UP...NOW!" His voice boomed throughout the bedroom causing me to jump.

"What the fuck is wrong with you, babe?"

"B, just please get up."

I did as I was told and followed him down the stairs. He opened the door for his mother, and I swear he turned into a bitch for her. Everything was yes mother this and yes mother that. She looked at me like I was beneath her. Unfortunately, this is my first time meeting her and Tank rarely speaks of her. From what I heard from Cookie, she likes to play on Tank's condition.

Taking a deep breath, I walked towards them to allow Tank to introduce me to her.

"Mom, I want you to meet my fiancée Bri..."

"Fiancée!" She quickly cut him off and cut her eyes towards me.

When she first walked in, I thought she was the prettiest woman I had ever seen. She was tall like them, maybe 5'11 smooth caramel skin tone, with not one blemish in sight. She had a cute blonde pixie cut. You can tell she was older, but her body was still bad as hell, like Angela Bassett. She wore this nice fitted pair of peach slacks that flared out at the leg with this cream sheer top loosely tucked in. Her neck and ears were drenched in diamonds.

Just by looking at her, you can clearly tell she had money. However, the look on her face made me turn my nose up real fucking quick at her snooty ass.

"Tank, you know you are not capable of finding a good woman. Your mind isn't even thinking properly. Do us both a favor and get rid of her. I will find you a nice wholesome girl." She rubbed the back of her hand across his cheek.

My mouth dropped to the floor. I stood there folding up my arms, just waiting on him to let her have it. Tank love me entirely too much to allow her or anyone to tell him to get rid of me.

148

"Yes, Mother!"

You would have thought I was the little girl in the movie *Exorcist* the way my head spun around when he said that shit.

"What the fuck you mean 'yes mother'? How you gone let this bitch come up in here and tell you what to do in OUR shit? You know what it's time for you to go."

Walking to the door, I swung it open so she can get her ass out. "This is my house and before I let you get into his head with bullshit, and I end up fucking you up, I'ma be respectful and tell you to get the fuck out."

"See Tremaine; this is what I am talking about. What type of woman will disrespect your mother like this?"

"This kind!" I spoke up, gesturing for her to leave.

She grabbed her things and walked out the door. Tank just stood there with this dumbfounded ass look on his face.

"British, I am really sorry about my mother. She likes to have control over Tank because she feels like Chase and I slipped away from her. She knows we are too strong to let her talk to us

149

like that. Don't worry! You did the right thing by telling her off, or every time she comes to visit she will disrespect your home." Cassie reached in for a hug and walked out behind her mother. I shut the door and walked towards Tank.

"Here you dropped these."

"What?"

"Your balls!" I looked at him right in his eyes so he could look at me and see how serious I was. "If you ever, ever, let her talk about me like I ain't shit again, we gone have a bigger problem than the one we have right now. You gone man the fuck up, and stop letting her get to you. This is yo shit, how dare she come in and act like she owns this motherfucker. My name is on this bitch and until she learns how to respect me, and respect my man, that bitch will be forever stuck on the outside of those gates. She will not be allowed in here. Now snap out of this shit and bring yo ass back to bed."

Walking away from him, I continued talking until I made it back to our room. "Coming over my house at seven o'clock in the morning on dummy shit. Hurry yo ass up!" I yelled over my

shoulder.  His ass really just pissed me all the way off.

# Chapter 17

## Chase

It seems like my life has been all over the place lately. I'm trying to get baby girl back to walking on her leg. She goes to physical therapy four times a week. After that shit had happened with British and her physical therapist, I refused to have a nigga in my house stretching my bitch out. I need them in front of people at all times. I'm sure he would rather lose his job than his life, any day. With Cookie out of commission, the girls have been calling on me a lot more now.

Every other day I have to fly somewhere. Not cause the guys aren't paying, but because the girls made so much money they don't want it just lying around while they are out of the room. I make sure I pick my shit up— quickly. Shit, on top of me traveling like crazy, I made time to go by Popeye's to see if they had a video but seems like it was already retrieved. I thought it was Tank, but when I asked him, he said he assumed it was me. Now we are back to square one with all of this.

"Hey baby, you wanna get out the house today?" I asked when I saw her in bed just staring at a blank screen.

"I'm not really in the mood today babe, I kinda just wanted to rest."

"You have been in this bed for days. Cookie, you have to move around if you wanna get better. On top of that, I'm sure Pops does not want to sit in the house and watch you all day. He's trying to get out and see what Miami has to offer him." She quickly turned her head towards me.

"What are you talking about, Chase?" Mr. B stepped inside of the room.

"Hey BG!" he spoke calling her the name he has called her since she was a kid.

When she heard his voice, she damn near broke her other leg trying to jump out the bed to get to him. She has not seen her father since the funeral, and I knew that would bring her out of this damn room.

"Aww, Chase! Thank you… thank you... thank you…" she planted wet kisses on my lips and moved as fast as her legs would allow towards her father.

"I will be back a little later to check on you guys."

I closed the room door and went downstairs to the kitchen. I needed Lucinda to hook me up one of those bomb ass sandwiches.

*RING… RING!*

*Shit, a nigga can't even get one moment to himself,* I thought to myself, trying to ignore the ringing of my phone. Once I pulled it out and saw it was my brother, I answered.

"What's good bruh?"

"Man bruh, you know I told you I don't trust that nigga Major right. Tell me why I just followed him and guess whose house he pulled up to."

"Boy, keep talking..."

"Charmaine!" Ain't this some shit, no wonder his ass ain't never around when shit happens. He's probably been setting her up.

"You know what we got for pussy niggas, right?" I stated

"I already called a meeting! See you at the warehouse."

I clicked the phone with Tank, grabbed my sandwich Lucinda made and headed out the door.

*** 

"What's good, where everybody at?" Major asked upon taking a seat in the only chair we had in the warehouse. "I know them niggas know you're punctual as hell and you like to start shit on time. So what's up? Y'all found them niggas who did that shit to the girls yet?"

For some reason, this nigga would not stop talking. He acted like he was nervous and trying to take the attention off of himself.

"Nah, actually we didn't. We figured you would come soon with some good news but for some reason…" I stopped before firing up a blunt. "…You haven't done shit."

"My bad about that, I've been…"

"Too busy fucking the enemy!" Tank shouted, right before he knocked Major ass out.

"Fuck Tank, I told yo ass to hit 'em but not knock him out. Now we gotta wait till this nigga wake up, to kill his ass."

"Damn that!" Tank stated and walked out the back of the warehouse only to return with a pair of Pliers.

I sat and watched my brother's eyes turn pitch black. He kneeled down and opened Major mouth; smacked him a few times to see if he would wake up. When he didn't, Tank turned into a fucking dentist and started pulling teeth. After the first three were pulled, Major woke up screaming out like a bitch.

"I was sitting here trying to figure out why you're getting paid for protecting a motherfucker you can't seem to protect. Here we are breaking good bread with yo ass, not that Kroger brand but that Sara Lee type bread with yo ass, and yet you don't do shit. First, we come home from the airport and get shot at, then the girls get rammed and pushed into traffic." Major tried to speak, but Tank was not hearing that shit at all.

"With each incident, you were nowhere to be found. Oh, and did I forget to mention that I searched your house earlier today when I saw you at Charmaine house and I found the tape from Popeyes."

I almost lost my fucking mind when he said that shit. I jumped up and ran over to him.

"You mean to tell me you had the tape the entire fucking time." I pulled my gun out and put it to his head.

"He didn't want us to see the tape cause he was sitting on the passenger side grinning like a Cheshire Cat. Muthafucka had the biggest smile known to fucking man plastered across his face, while our girls were calling us for help."

"Tank, you're doing too much talking. Fuck this!"

BOOM! BOOM!

"Call somebody to clean this shit up. We're gone catch up to Charmaine ass tomorrow. I gotta get back to Cookie."

I walked outside, jumped into my whip, and hurried home. I had a big evening planned for Pops. I hope he like football cause I got us some tickets to see the Miami Dolphins play. Pulling up into the driveway, Pops and Cookie were sitting on the swing that I had hanging from a tree.

I remember her telling me about her summer visits to her great-grandparents house in McComb, Ms. They had this swing attached to this old tree in the front yard that she and her cousins used to fight over. She came home one day from shopping with British, and both of their asses started crying when they saw the swing. I had her dad send me a picture of the swing, and I had my guy make an exact replica of it for her.

"It's about time you showed up baby; I thought I had to entertain this old man by myself." She nudged him and started smiling at me.

"No baby, I have something planned for him. Be ready by five o'clock old man," I joked and made my way to my room.

Before I got half way up the stairs, my phone started buzzing with a text.

***WIFEY: CHANGE YA FUCKING SHIRT, BABY!***

Shit, I'm slipping for real. I had Major blood splatter on the bottom of my shirt. I rushed into the room to jump in the shower to get dressed for the game.

# Chapter 18

# Swamp

*BAM! BAM! BAM!*

"Open this motherfucking door bitch. I know he up in there laid up with yo hoe ass.

*BAM! BAM! BAM!*

"Bitch you better open up before I kick this bitch in." I continued to beat on the door until the door swung open and she had a .9mm pointed to my face.

"Sammy don't come to my house with this bullshit. What the fuck are you talking about?"

"Do not pay with me, Charm. I know Major is in there with you. He did not come by yesterday and his damn clothes are all over my house. HE NEEDS TO COME GET HIS SHIT NOW!" I spat, jumping up and down trying to see past her.

"Baby, who's at the door?" A man came up behind her half-naked and kissed on her neck. He was fine as hell; his body was looking like he was made specifically for me. Tattoos covered the majority of his arms. My nature started to rise just looking at him. After my eyes roamed his body, I finally looked at his face; he had nice pink full lips, caramel skin tone, with some smooth ass waves in his low cut fade, making me want to go deep sea diving in them and in him— if you know what I mean. Just looking at him made the inner bitch come out of me. I damn near wanted to high five Charm for pulling this nigga, like YAASSSS BIIIHHHH YAAASSS! But, I had to keep my composure cause I still wanted to know where Major ass was.

"It's just my little brother, Swamp."

He looked at me, and his eyes had me stuck; they were this extra light hazel color and matched so well with his skin tone. I didn't know if I was supposed to say hey or just stare at him. Either way, I enjoyed the staring idea way more. He shifted his eyes from me and looked back at my sister.

"Make it quick; I'm not done with you yet." Kissing her on the back of her head, he turned and walked away.

"Damn bitch, you move fast," I whispered making sure he did not hear me.

"Girl hush, anyway I gotta go your lil' man is not here. I saw him briefly yesterday just to discuss some business, but after that, he left."

"Ok, I will try a few more places before I burn up all his shit. Go back in the house and enjoy that meat," I joked, turning to walk back to my car.

I know Major is around here somewhere and once I get my hands on him, it's gone be hell to pay because my house is not a damn storage. Pulling off from Charm house, I decided to ride around a little bit to see if I will run into him. I would hate to do a pop up at that warehouse he be at. One day I followed him there thinking he was going to fuck off, but he was meeting the guy Charm used to work for. At first, I was a little skeptical. I know him and Charm hooking up wasn't a coincidence. She was just using his ass to get to Chase since I dropped the ball. It's cool; he can be a little pawn in her game of lies.

\*\*\*

I walked into the mall to find me something to wear to this lil' all white party I heard about. I needed something simple but

162

sexy, something gay, but still showed I was into bitches to just in case they wanted to try the kid out too.

I walked past the window of DSW and saw this girl standing next to an older lady trying on shoes. She was gorgeous, a toasted almond complexion, long jet black hair, nice tight body. her dimples started to show when she smiled at the lady she was with. She turned around to take a seat in the chair to try the new Jessica Simpson, 2017 summer collection limited edition snakeskin red heel on zher foot. As she sat down our eyes locked, as bad as I wanted to move away so I would not stare at her, my feet just would not move. Then it hit me; it was the same girl I saw at my guy Turk house.

"So are you just going to stand here and stare at my daughter or go inside and introduce yourself to her," the lady that once was standing next to the girl inside the store was now standing next to me stated, pulling my attention away.

"I'm sorry, I wasn't trying to stare. I didn't mean any disrespect by it. She's just so beautiful and caught my eyes as I was walking pass."

163

The lady stood about 5'11, caramel skin, her hair was in this blonde pixie cut style. She was older but still carried herself like a younger woman. You can tell by the body suit top she wore, paired with skinny jeans that hugged every inch of her curves, with a pair of Christian Louboutin heels.

"It's ok, trust me! You should go in and speak to her, and don't act like you don't want to. I saw you drooling from the inside." She laughed and walked off from me.

I turned to walk into the store. As I approached her, she looked even more beautiful than when I saw her the first time.

"I see my mom suckered you into coming inside," she stated right when I walked up to her.

"I wouldn't call it suckered, she just simply told me to stop drooling and get my ass inside."

She started laughing, and her smile made my heart skip a beat. I think I just found the future Mrs. Sammie 'Swamp' August.

"I'm Sammie, nice to meet you." She looked at me and smiled before reaching her hand out.

"I'm Cassie, nice to meet you as well." I took a seat next to her. The more and more we talked the more I wanted to get down on my knees and ask her to marry me. She goes to one of the universities here for fashion and design. She has two older brothers, and her dad died a few years ago. I wanted to sit and listen to her talk all night; her voice was so soft and pleasant. Time had gotten away from us, it was two hours later, and we were still sitting inside the shoe store talking. I'm not sure where her mom went, but she must have known her daughter was in good hands because she has not returned yet.

"I'm not sure why, but just talking to you and laughing with you makes me feel like we have known each other forever. I would love to see you again," I stated as we started walking to the front so she could purchase her shoes.

"That will not be a problem at all, here's my number." She handed me a business card. *Cassandra Williams, Fashion and Design,* is what the card said with a pretty ass picture of her on the front.

"That will be $217.84," the cashier said.

While we were talking, she kept trying on shoes and every one I said she looked good in she had sat those to the side. I didn't know she was going to purchase each pair. She reached for her card, but I stopped her.

"Let me get this for you. It's my token of appreciation just for you even taking the time out to talk to me." She smiled and stepped aside. I could feel her standing there taking in all of me. "You know you don't have to stare at me right."

"I know, but I just wanted you to see how it felt when you were out there staring at me." She smiled and tilted her head slightly to the right. I swear this girl is about to have me wrapped around her finger; I needed to make her mine. Grabbing her bags off the counter, we walked out of the store. Her mom was sitting at the food court on the phone, so I walked her over to her.

"It took y'all long enough! I thought you would be quicker than that with asking for her number. You had me sitting out here with these broke ass people. I swear I had to clutch my purse and my pearls several times thinking one of these hoodlums were going to snatch my shit." She laughed and locked arms with Cassie. They both were some beautiful women; I definitely can see where she got her looks from.

"My bad, the time just kinda slipped away from us. I will let you all enjoy the rest of your evening. I'm going to call you, later on tonight; maybe we can do dinner."

"She would love that!" Her mom spoke up before she could even say anything. "Call her around seven o'clock; she will be ready." And with that, she turned her around and walked away.

Cassie turned her head back around to me as they walked off and gave me that sexy ass smile of her. *Shit, that girl is gone be the death of me,* I thought to myself as I walked away with my nose wide open.

# Chapter 19

## Cassandra "Cassie" Williams

I could not believe how my mother was acting. She practically threw me to Sammie like I was a piece of meat. If he wasn't so damn fine, I would have been pissed. Sammie looked like he was mixed with black and some other shit. Despite the fact his hair is longer than mine, I can still fuck with him. Those men with long hair and dreads sling that shit harder than females with fresh 32' bundles and have you side eyeing the hell out of them. He seems really cool though. He's 22 years old, the same age I am, and a lot different from the men I usually choose. I typically go for men with buff bodies, long beards, tattoos covering his entire upper body, with a big ass missile in his pants. He was the opposite of that. When I say opposite, I mean TOTAL opposite. He looked a little goofy, but he had swag with it.

My mom knows exactly how my relationships are. I believe that's why she was so quick to push me off on him. For her, I will step outside of the norm, and see where it gets me. But, this lil' man got one time to put his hands on me like my last guy did and I'm calling my brothers on his ass.

"He seemed like a nice guy, right pooh?" my mom asked right when I sat down in her car.

"Yea ma, he seems nice."

"You deserve someone way better than that damn thug you been talking to. What's his name? Mickey… Yea Mickey. How you gone be a thug and put yo hands on a woman, and you got a name like Mickey?"

My mom can be a bit much at times, but for once, she does have a point. I believe that's why he hit women. Because his name is so soft, he feels he has to prove himself. I'm sure he learned his lesson when Tank put his ass in the hospital how he did me.

Being the only sister of two well-known men, you would think he would have known not to put his hands on me. He had to learn the hard way though.

"Let's go home and get you all dolled up. I'm sure this man will be full of surprises for you. I could look at him and tell he was

169

really feeling you. The way that boy stopped at that window and admired my little angel, made mama smile."

Lord, please be some ear plugs right now because she will not stop talking.

***

*BEEP!*

A text came through my phone right when I got out of the shower.

***305-423-0947: Wear something sexy. After you get dressed, send me your address. I can't wait to see your beautiful face again. -Sammie***

Once I read the text, this big grin quickly spread across my face. I was hoping he didn't stand me up because I refused to Netflix and Chill with mama for the third time this week. She wanted so badly to stay at my place until I got dressed but I brushed that idea out of her head, how Chicago from *Poetic Justice*, brushed his weak ass fade. She was not about to embarrass me again. She needs her some good meat in her life, and maybe she will get out of mine.

**ME: Same here, 439 Miami Shore Drive.**

I tossed my phone on the bed and walked across the hall into my second bedroom that I made into a walk in closet. He said to wear something sexy, so I started pulling out all of the tight dresses I could find. I was throwing, Gucci here, Prada there, until my eyes landed on my Hunter Green Bodycon dress by Armani. It was off the shoulders, and the back of the dress was cut out into a diamond shape, exposing my artwork on my lower back. I paired it with a pair of beige Jimmy Choo heels that were embellished with little diamonds around the ankle strap. I don't mind mixing up designers as long as it looks good together.

Once I put it on, that damn dressed hugged me like it missed me. My ass was poking out just right, and my girls were sitting real pretty too. I always wear my hair straight, but tonight I decided to do it a little different. I had my friend Krystal come over, do my makeup, and put some body wave loose curls in my hair. I stood there in the mirror and admired myself. For once, I

171

could look at myself as this beautiful person everyone saw me as. Mickey had my self-esteem so low, at one point I did not care what I looked like coming out of the house as long as I was with him. I had no one else to impress so whatever made him happy I wore it.

*SNIFF! SNIFF!*

I turned around to see my best friend standing behind me with tears in her eyes.

"Cass, you look absolutely gorgeous. Any man would be lucky to have you on his arm right now. I have not seen you look this good, in so long. I missed this old you, this person standing right in front of me. I've missed her, and I'm so glad you are back to your old self again. I hope this guy you are going out with tonight treats you just like the queen you are. I love you, boo." She wrapped her arms around my neck, and the tears started to flow.

"Now you know you're gone have to redo my makeup, right!" We laughed, and I walked back over to the chair.

"Girl… hush! I will do it 100 times over, as long as I can see this smile on your face over and over again."

Moments later, I heard my doorbell ring. She peeped out the window and said it was a candy apple red Lexus in my driveway. I stood up, adjusted my dress and walked to the door, taking a deep breath before I pulled the door open.

"Hey handso… damn, you look good!"

I couldn't believe I just said that, but Sammie didn't look like the Sammie I met earlier in the mall. He had on this gray suit, not your old fashion gray suit but the slim fit kind, with this gray and white stripe button up, a dark gray tie, and a gray vest that match the pants. Honestly, he looked like he just stepped off the top of a wedding cake, but something about the way he wore it made that shit look good. His hair was now braided into two long braids; it looked like he just stepped out of the barber's chair before he got out the car.

I heard him chuckle, which pulled me from just staring at him.

"You wanna invite me in, or are we just going to play the staring game."

"I'm sorry, you can come in. Just let me grab my purse, and we can be on the way out. Oh, this is my best friend Krystal, she was just leaving."

I pushed her out the door before she could start asking him 21 questions on if he has a friend, brother, or cousin for her. Grabbing my clutch off the bed, we then headed out the door.

"I hope you like my surprise," he stated while grabbing my hand and walking me to his car.

Once he got in, I had to look at him again. I was sitting there smiling and blushing at him like a high school schoolgirl whose crush had just spoken to her for the first time. The butterflies quickly took over my stomach, and I became nervous. I haven't been on a date in a long time, and I just hope I don't say the wrong thing. Sometimes my mouth can be like my mama's, and I know that will make this go sour real quick.

He reached over and grabbed my hand as we drove down the expressway. We pulled up to this tall building and took the elevator all the way up. Sammie was just standing across from me staring me up and down.

"You really are beautiful," he finally spoke, making me blush.

"Thank you. You're not so bad yourself." The elevator doors opened up to the rooftop.

"I hope you're not afraid of heights." With that said a helicopter came down and landed.

The closer we got to the helicopter, the more my hair started flying all over the places. I was pissed off because she really did a good job on my hair and now it was ruined. He helped me inside and took a seat next to me. I think he saw I was irritated because of my hair.

"Don't worry about your hair, if I have to, I will pay for it to get done again. You still look good, minus this piece sticking up right here." He laughed and moved the piece of hair down, handed me some ear things to put on, and we were off. I know Miami is beautiful, but it is even more beautiful from up in the sky. I was so amazed at him to even think of something like this. I had never been in a helicopter before, and if it weren't for him, I would have never thought of it.

175

After about 20 minutes of touring the city, we landed on top of another building. The driver opened the door for us, and he handed him a tip. It was a red carpet stretched out that lead to a single dinner table. I smiled so hard after seeing that. He was really making me feel special. I grabbed his face and gave him the biggest kiss ever.

"Sammie, this is so romantic. I have never done anything like this before."

"As long as you are with me, every day will be different. I don't want to be anything like your ex. Whether he was good to you or bad to you, I only strive to be me. I, Sammie August, will always give you more than the usual."

Placing several kisses on the back of my hand, he then pulled my chair out for me. Someone came out the door with a bottle of wine, and then another came out with dinner. We sat there and talked about everything, but our past. He wasn't interested in it. He said he was only concerned about the future and all the different ways he can make me smile every day.

It was starting to get late, and as much as I did not want this night to end, my bed was calling my name. We walked over to the elevator that took us to the lobby of the building where his car was now waiting for us there.

"I really had a great time with you tonight."

"Don't worry; this will be the first of many great times."

He locked hands with mine and continued to drive me home. Doing just as a gentleman does, he got out, opened the door for me, and walked me to my door.

"Hope to see you soon," I stated as I put my key into the door and pushed it open.

"No doubt mama, it'll be sooner than you think. We have only just begun!"

He pulled me back out of the door and kissed me. The kisses were so passionate that I literally felt my soul leave my body, and I was floating on cloud 9. Stumbling trying to catch my balance once he let me go, he had my knees weak. Now I see how SWV felt.

"See you later, beautiful."

"See you later, handsome" I turned and walked into the house.

I took my dress off as quick as I could and laid across my bed. After laying and looking up at the ceiling thinking about him and that kiss he just gave me, I rolled over and opened my nightstand drawer.

I need this thang on turbo mode

BUZZZZZZ... BUZZZZZZZZ... BUUUZZZZZZ!

The vibrations from my toy had me in another world, and all I could picture was riding Sammie backwards while he gripped my waist.

"HMMMMM... SHIIITTT!"

There is nothing my trusty rabbit couldn't fix. After I had put my toy away, a text came through my phone.

**BEEP!**

*SAM: Good night, beautiful.*

*ME: Good night, handsome.*

# Chapter 20

## British

I walked into this store called Party and Paper to find some more things for Cookie's baby shower. She already has everything; Chase made sure of that. I decided to have her a diaper shower where the guest only brings diapers and wipes. If they choose to bring more that's fine too. I invited her dad, of course, a few of the girls that I know she talks to on the regular. Like Tonya, Marie, Toys, Keshia, Paris, and a few others.

"Hello, do you need help with anything?"

"Oh no, I just needed to grab a few more table covers and balloons," I replied to the associate, She would bring her ass over here and ask if I need anything after I walked this entire store. Making my way to the register, I checked out and grabbed my things.

*What the hell is this?* I thought to myself, reaching for the paper that was on my windshield.

*Enjoy my husband while you can, he won't be with you for long.*

"What the fuck is this shit? They must have the wrong car!" I said aloud. Getting inside the car, the first thing I did was call up Tank.

"Hey, baby."

"Is there something you need to tell me?" I questioned right when he answered the phone.

"Besides, I love you? No… why?"

"I'm just wondering because I was leaving out of the store and it was a note stuck to my window."

"Was it a ticket? You know yo ass stay parking in the wrong area." He laughed, but I didn't find shit funny.

"No, actually it was a note from your wife!" His laugh stopped suddenly.

"B, what the fuck are you talking about? I don't have a wife."

"Tank, for your safety and hers, I hope you don't. I have been through entirely too much with you. We are finally at a happy place, and I don't want it ruined by some ex that can't seem to get over you."

"Baby, you have nothing to worry about." He kept trying to assure me that everything was good.

"See you when I get home." I clicked the phone and did the dash to Cookie's house to drop off the rest of the things.

When I got there, Toys was already there. She's starting to come around a lot lately. I talk to her, but I really don't talk to her. It just seems odd how she just appeared out the blue and now all of a sudden she's clinging to Cookie like a fat bitch in spandex.

"Hey, y'all," I spoke stepping out on the back patio where they were sitting.

"Hey cousin, what are you doing here?"

"Just dropping the last of the things off for the shower. What are y'all doing?"

"I stopped by to give her my gifts; I won't make the shower." Toys spoke.

That's a relief; I was only being nice by inviting her anyway. She hasn't done anything to me, but like I said she just seem a little odd to me.

"I'm going to leave now and let you two ladies talk. Oh British, make sure you get your balloon and bear I got for you. I dropped it off here after the accident. If I had known where you lived, it would have been easier to just drop it off to you." *Nope, you did the right thing, lil' bitch does not need to know my address,* I thought to myself.

"Thanks, I will get it when I leave out."

She gave me this fake ass hug. I was frowning up and looking down at Cookie. She was looking right in my face shaking her head. Cookie knows I don't be quick to fuck with new people. Toys left from the back, and I took a seat next to Cookie.

"You know yo ass can be mean, why did you frown yo nose up like that at her?"

"I don't know what it is, but I just don't trust her. How did you say you guys met again?"

She went into details about the night Tank had one of his episodes and beat the hell out of me. Shots started going off in the club and Toys came in like a bitch in shining armor, and Gucci pumps to save her.

"I guess girl, anyway look at this." I handed her the note that was on my car.

"What's this?"

"A note that was stuck to my damn window today. I swear Cookie if this man is married, I'm killing him."

"Stop it, B! You know Tank loves your crazy ass, and he would never do anything to hurt you— on purpose anyway. Whoever it was probably had the wrong car, so calm down before you do or say the wrong thing."

"I hear you. Anyway, I need to get home so I can talk to Tank face to face. See you first thing in the morning." I gave her a hug and went back inside.

"Hey Lucinda, I hope you're ready to work tomorrow cause I have a lot of shit to put up," I announced to the maid on my way out the door.

"What the fuck!" Walking around my car, I saw all of my tires were on flat. First, it's the note and now this shit. Pulling my phone out, I called call Tank.

"Hello."

"Get yo ass to Chase's house, right now!"

"British, who the fuck are you talking to like that?" He yelled.

"Nigga I'm talking to you. Somebody put my damn tires on flat, and I'm starting to think this shit is intentional."

"B, you better calm yo ass down for real, I'll be there in a second!" He clicked the phone before I could say anything back.

Stepping back from my car, I couldn't do anything but look at my car and shake my head. This is some bullshit.

I walked back into the house and sat back outside with Cookie.

185

"I thought you were leaving?" she questioned as I walked through the patio doors.

"Shit... me too! I'm waiting on Tank to pick me up. Somebody flattened my tires."

"What? Are you sure?"

"Bitch, fuck you mean am I sure! I have flattened enough tires in my day to know what they look like. Stop it! I don't get it Cook; I don't fuck with nobody, I don't go out unless I'm with you. The only people I kick it with are you, sometimes the girls, and my man.

First, it was the note which I looked at that as they put it on the wrong car, but now this."

I was starting to get really frustrated, and Tank ass is not getting here fast enough. My mind started racing trying to figure out when someone had time to slash my damn tires. I wasn't inside the store long enough for them to slash them there on top of that, I would have felt it when I started driving. Then I came right here,

Cookie's gates are closed so they couldn't have followed me here, Unless… "Toys!" I blurted out, causing Cookie to jump.

"Girl, you scared the shit out of me. What the hell are you calling her name out for?"

"Because that bitch had to be the one to flatten my damn tires. I swear if it's her Cookie, I'm fucking her up on sight for real."

"Nah, it can't be her! Why would she do something like that? She never acted like she had an issue with you, she even bought you a get well balloon with a bear inside."

Shaking my head back and forth, "Well, I better not pop it open cause that bitch could be laced with anthrax." Cookie started busting up laughing. I didn't find it funny. I was simply telling the truth.

"Come here, British!" Tank snared, looking at me with evil eyes. We walked out front to look at my tires. "Did you see anyone following you?" Standing there with an attitude and my arms folded.

"No Tank, if I did I would have told yo ass someone was following me. Duh!" The next thing I know he rushed over to my face.

"B, you gone lose this funky ass attitude you got. I'm over here trying to help you. I don't know who did this shit and why it was done, but you're mad at the wrong motherfucker. Fix that attitude before I fix it for you," he spoke through clenched teeth, just inches from my face.

"Boooy, if you don't back the hell up out my face. Yea I have an attitude. Some bitch slashed my tires. You think I supposed to be happy about this bullshit?" By this time, Cookie had stepped outside to see what's going on. "My shit wasn't fucked up until I got to Cookie house and her bestie was here."

"Girl stop, that is not my bestie!" Cookie corrected.

"Who is her bestie?" Tank asked.

"Some bitch name Toys."

"You think she did this?"

"Yes Tank, I do! She left before I did and this was not like this when I got here. Now unless Lucinda's ass came out here and fucked my shit up because I keep asking her to make me sandwiches then yes, I think it was Toys."

"We can figure this shit out right now. I will tell Chase to pull his security cameras, and we can settle this." Tank spoke, walking pass Cookie to get inside the house.

We sat outside and waited on them to finish pulling the footage. After about 30 minutes, Tank burst through the front doors.

"Let's go!"

"But I haven't looked at the…"

Clinching his fist tight, he screamed, "I said let's go, NOW!" causing me to jump up immediately.

"Tank, you need to calm down and tell me what's wrong."

"We will talk when we get home. Just get in, and I'll have my guy come fix your car later."

I got inside the car, and we headed home. The entire ride was silent; I didn't know what was going through Tank's head. I was pissed because I wanted to see if it was Toys bitch ass who cut my tires, but Tank ruined that by making me leave.

Pulling up at the house, we just sat there a while before getting outside.

"I need to talk to you about something." *Ah, hell here we go,* I thought to myself. I sat there trying to mentally prepare myself for what he wanted to tell me.

# Chapter 21

## Cassie

*DING DONG!*

*DING DONG!*

I really wanted to sleep past nine o'clock today, but I see my mother is out early since it's only seven. My bell never rings this early unless it's her ass trying to see how my night went. Grabbing my silk robe from my bathroom door, I threw it on and headed to the door.

*DING DONG!*

*DING DONG!*

"Hold on shit. I'm coming!" I yelled out getting really annoyed. Swinging the door open with the meanest mug I could muster up on my face.

"Are you Cassie Williams?" the lady asked upon me opening the door.

"Yes, I am."

"These are for you." The young lady handed me a dozen of rainbow colored roses. They were absolutely gorgeous, and my mug turned into a smile quick as hell when I saw the flowers. I reached my arm out to grab them and gave 'em a little sniff. I've always heard that roses really smell like boo boo, so I had to check before I brought them into my house.

"Thank you," I stated before turning away from the door, so I could hurry up and read the card that was attached. I placed the vase in the center of my dining room table and removed the card. *Day 1 of me making sure every day with me is better than your last. Be dressed by 5. - Sammie*

I had the biggest grin on my face after reading the card. It was simple but so cute at the same time. Pouring me up a cup of coffee, I sat down at the table and just started thinking about our night. From the helicopter ride to dinner on the rooftop, everything was perfect. Usually, all my dates consist of him stunting, trying to show me how much money he has, how many trips he takes, what he can do for me— you know the usual bullshit.

My last guy was the worst, he used to go on this power trip, and if I didn't listen to him, he quickly showed me who the man was in the relationship. One day I got tired of it and told my brothers. I just could not deal with being his punching bag every time we got into an argument or disagreed about something simple. I remember once. We got into it because I ordered lemon pepper wings.

*DING DONG!*

*DING DONG!*

"Who is it?"

"Girl, open this damn door up!" Taking a deep breath, I opened the door.

"Soooo, how was your night? Where did you go? How much did he spend on you?" My mom came right in being nosy.

For once, I wanted to keep something private because once she knows about it, for some reason things start to go downhill for me, especially, if they do not meet her standards. My mom means well, but sometimes she can be a bit overbearing.

"Everything was great Ma; we had a nice time." I tried to give her as less info as possible. She walked over to the table once she saw the flowers sitting there and started reading the card.

"Well, what are you waiting on, get dressed!" I must have looked at her like she lost all of her mind. First off, it's now close to eight a.m., and the card says five.

"Ma, I'm sorry but you gotta go, and I'm going back to bed. I will get dressed when it's time. Go… go… go…" Pushing her out of the door, I wish I ran into a fine ass old man cause I would be hooking her ass up with him right about now.

Walking back towards my bed, I jumped in and covered my head with the covers. I don't want to do anything right now but sleep.

*BEEP!*

"Uggghhh!!!" I screamed out while kicking up and down in the air. Rolling over, I grabbed my phone off the nightstand to read the text.

*SAMMIE: Just wanted you to know I was thinking about you and five o'clock is too long to see you again.*

Awww this nigga is really trying to get in the panties.

*ME: I know, I wish I could see you sooner as well. I was lying down, but my nosy ass mama came over here bother me.*

*SAMMIE: Lol, she seems like a nice lady.*

*ME: Only when she wanna be. Oh, and thank you for the flowers, they are so beautiful.*

*SAMMIE: They were picked with you in mind.*

*SAMMIE: You know what scratch that five o'clock. Get dressed, let's meet up now. We can do breakfast and after that, maybe something fun. So dress comfortably.*

*ME: Yes sir, lol... See you soon.*

All of a sudden, my tiredness went away. I was ready to see my lil' dip with his fine ass. I went into my closet and pulled out a jogging Nike outfit I have with some Nike Air Max 95. Instead of having my hair down how I usually wear it, I decided to wear it in a high ponytail, sprayed on some of my Victoria Secret Very Sexy

195

perfume and headed out the door. He sent me a text asking me to meet him at IHOP, and I was happy as shit cause my thick ass has been craving pancakes for a while. I turned my Apple Music radio on from my phone and rushed over to meet him.

*** 

"Where do you want to go next?" Sammie questioned, once we finished our breakfast.

We had a nice talk trying to get to know each other more. He's an Engineering major, finishing up his last year. He has an older sister, and for some reason, he looked kind of funny in the face when he mentioned her. I have to make sure to ask him about that later. But right now he's trying to go and do something else and honestly, my ass wants to go lay back down, but I said I would do something fun, so I guess I will keep my word.

"I'm down to do whatever, surprise me like you did last night."

"You're no fun; I wanted you to surprise me this time. What's something that you have always wanted to do, but haven't?"

"Hmm, I have always wanted go skydiving, or hike up a mountain, or horseback riding on a beach, or zip lining."

"Yo ass watch too much white folks shit. Don't no niggas do shit like that."

"Well, Mr. Sammie August it looks like we're about to be the first niggas that do then. You said you wanted me to plan something this time, sooo... " I stated while scrolling through my phone to find us something to do. "Got it... let's go!" He paid the tab, and I threw the tip on the table "Leave your car here; I will bring you back, later on, to pick it up.

We got into my car and headed right over to Miami Skydiving Center. I was nervous as hell but wanted to show his ass I had an adventurous side.

"Babe, so out of all the things you named you wanted to do, this is the one you decided on?" Sammie asked, looking up at the sign.

"Yo ass wanted adventure so don't get scared now. Get that ass out and let's have some fun," I said playfully, knowing my ass was scared as fuck too.

He grabbed my hand, and we walked inside. Giving him a once over, I licked my lips at how sexy he looked standing here looking like he could model for Jordan clothing line. He wore some black Jordan sweats, a white Tee, and a pair of Low Jordan Retro 11s. He made the simplest fit look fly as hell. I was still slick jealous at his hair being longer than mine.

"What you over there thinking about?" he asked, pulling my attention back towards his face.

"Just you, it's crazy we just met yesterday, but it feels like we have been knowing each other for a while. Everything about you is different from my ex. From the way you walk, talk, the types of date you chose to take me on. I haven't smiled this much

in years. Honestly, I can't wait to see what tomorrow will bring."
He pulled me in close to him and kissed me on my forehead.

"No need to speak on your past situationships. I'm not them. I told you in the note this morning that I wanted to make every day better than you last. I didn't say that just to be saying it. I'm cut from a totally different cloth. Mine is made of silk on one side and and steel on the other.

Depending on who I'm around determines what side of me you will get. Now, don't get me wrong, I'm far from a soft ass man. I just know how to tend to a woman's needs. Sometimes they want you to be gentle, compassionate, loving and sometimes they want that pressure," he stated, stepping into my space. "Just look at me like the guy from the Allstate commercial, you're in good hands with me."

He reached down, grabbed my hand, pulled it up to his mouth and gave me one of those soft, sexy kisses on the back. I felt a tingling sensation flow through my coochie that made me immediately cross my legs together.

"Cassie!" the attendant called out. "You're up next."

They started helping us put on all of our safety gear and walked us to the plane. I think Sammie must have felt my nervousness taking over my body because he grabbed hold of my hand and pulled me in the plane. I don't know why my ass didn't find something that was on the ground to do. Sitting there with my hands gripped tight to the seat, we took off. I felt my heart drop into my stomach as we made our way further up.

"You ready, babe?" Sammie asked as we interlocked arms.

"You want me to be honest, or lie?"

He laughed before responding. "What type of question is that? Yes, Patrice, I want you to be honest," calling me by my middle name.

"I'm scared shitless; is it too late to change our minds?"

"Hell yea it too late, we already up and the only way down is to jump. Don't worry, we jumping together, I'll make sure you're behind me so when we land, I can catch you if you fall." He leaned in and gave me the most passionate kiss known to mankind.

As we pulled away, the instructor that was with us pulled the door open and motioned for us to get up. After giving us our instructions, he waited a little while longer before telling us when to jump. It took everything in me not to shed a tear right then. My palms were sweaty, and my legs were trembling, but when I felt Sammie give my hand a gentle squeeze, a sense of calm came over me.

Looking at him, I gave him a weak smile, trying to remain calm and with that, the countdown began.

"1...2...3..." the instructor called out, and we jumped.

I felt a rush of excitement come over me; I couldn't believe I was doing this. Sammie was holding on to my hand so tight. He motioned for me to pull my parachute first then he followed right behind me. The view was so beautiful. After overcoming my fears, I was glad I did this and with someone who actually wanted be here with me. As long as I was happy, he was good with whatever. I just pray this thing stay how it is because I think I'm falling for him.

We both fell to the ground at the same time. Once we got back to the building and took our things off, he grabbed my face again and kissed me. I'm usually not a kisser, but for him, I'll tongue kiss his ass all the way to China and back if I had to.

"Let's go before you make me do something to yo sexy ass," he mumbled and bit his bottom lip.

# Chapter 22

## Cookie

After dealing with British and her drama, I wanted some alone time with my man, but his ass is forever going out of town on me. I understand his job sometimes requires him to travel but three and four times a week is a bit much, especially when you have a woman seven months pregnant at home. I'm finally getting back to walking regularly, and I want to get out of this house and just enjoy him for a change.

It has been days, and I have rarely seen him. He comes home late and leaves early. I don't know what's going on, but it is starting to feel like these walls are closing in on me. His phone is constantly going off, and of course, his ass will leave out the room like he is trying to hide something from me. Chase and I have never been here before. We have always just had to deal with other people problems but none of our own. Everything he tells me I hang on every word, and I just hope he is not using that to his advantage. That and the fact that I choose not to leave the house much anymore because it's too much shit going on.

Standing up and looking out of my window, I see him standing outside on the phone. I wanted so badly to eavesdrop on his conversation. "Fuck it!" I went over to the intercom and pressed outside. The speakers outside picked up, and I was able to hear what he was saying.

"Nah, you're good ma! She ain't leaving out the house no time soon. Especially after that little issue she had. She is exactly where I need her to be, in the house so I can know where she is at all times. You're still in Atlanta, right? Aight cool! I will catch a flight out tonight." He clicked the phone and headed inside the house.

My heart was beating uncontrollably, and I was so hurt. I could not believe he is about to go cheat on me. On top of that, he expects me just to sit here while he goes out and do wrong. Once I heard him coming into the room, I decided not to say anything about what I overheard. He promised he was different and I see he is just like the rest, for real. That good faithful man was not going to stick around long before the true him showed up. I knew he couldn't work around all these freak hoes and not want to fuck them.

"Hey baby, you finally decided to get out of bed?"

I quickly wiped the tear away that threatened to fall and turned around towards him. He really just came in here like nothing is going on and that made me get even madder.

"Yea, I'm up! What were you downstairs doing? You got out the bed early this morning."

"I had to handle a few things; I will be flying out tonight to handle some business. Don't you worry though, I promise not to be gone long, and I will be back in time to help you put up everything from your baby shower. So, once I am done, I will catch a flight right back home to you and my babies."

Stepping into my space, he rubbed his hands around my stomach as he kneeled down to talk to the boys. He always does this right before he leaves out the house.

"I really wish you would stay here with me; I haven't seen much of you lately. You are always running off here or there, and

I'm just stuck here with Lucinda's nonspeaking English ass." I don't know if it was the babies that had me emotional, but the tears started to escape from my eyes.

"London, listen to me, there's no other place I would rather be than with you. Since you are not coming out the house much, it is my job to handle the girls. I just need you to rest up and get prepared for the boys to arrive."

"Where are you going?"

"Just out of town to handle some business."

"I know that but where?" He kissed me on my forehead and sure enough, just as fast as he came in, he left out even faster.

The nigga never did answer my question, that is how I know he gotta be fucking a bitch. He just scared my ass gone do a pop up like British did on Tank ass. But that ain't in me; I'm not about to hop a flight for my man. If he wanna go be with another bitch then go right ahead. Just don't get mad when I drop these babies and start doing the shit too.

Right when I heard his car start up, I watched as he got half way down the driveway before I ran to my closet and started throwing clothes into my suitcase. I just wanted to get away for a little while. I wanted him to see how it feels to come home to nobody. Sitting in this house all day long is driving me insane. He spends more time with them girls than he does with me. After getting everything I needed, I grabbed my keys and my bags, made my way to the car, and left.

Pulling out of the driveway, I could have punched myself for always having my damn car on E. I never want to stop for gas, so I leave it like that so Chase can fill it up for me. I went around the corner and went inside for gas and some snacks to hold me over until I make it to Boca Raton. I don't have a clue what's there but I know, no one will look for me there.

The store was packed, and it took me forever to get back outside. I tried to get out of town before Chase showed up. I pumped my gas and jumped into the car. *Boca Raton, here I come,* I thought to myself. Turning on my girl Mary with her non-dancing ass, I cruised to the entire *Strength of a Woman* album. I looked online and booked me a hotel on the drive up here. Once I pulled in, I damn near jumped out cause I had to piss so damn bad. These boys were playing football with my bladder.

*CLICK!*

"I want you to get out this car and act normal. If you try to make one false move, I'ma do your ass how you did me— shoot you and leave you for dead."

My heart started pounding when I heard his voice. It was a voice I thought I would never hear again. At this moment, I was kicking my own ass for not making sure his ass was dead. "Do you understand me?" he said through clenched teeth.

"Yes Brandon, I understand please don't hurt me I'm preg…"

"You think I give a damn about you being pregnant. That lil' motherfucker ain't mine, now get yo ass out."

He climbed over the seat and slid out on the driver side right behind me, making sure he stayed close so his gun would be hidden. I tried to remain calm and think of a way to talk him out of this once we get inside the room.

How the fuck did I end up here? I should have stayed my stupid ass in the damn house. That big ass house I have, I could have just gone into another room for space. But nooo, crazy ass London wanted to go to another city and allow her crazy ass ex to get inside her car. Come to think of it, how the fuck did he get in my shit anyway?

Approaching the front desk, I tried to look at the attendant to signal I was in danger but this bitch is sitting her ass on the phone laughing and talking loud like she didn't see me here.

"Are you checking in or nah?" she asked, causing me to look at her sideways.

"Yes, I'm checking in."

I was raising my eyebrows every kind of way. I even tried winking at her doing whatever I could to get some help. She would not get the hint and just kept looking at me like I was crazy.

"Look, lady. I'm not with that gay shit so you can stop all that winking and shit at me. What's your name so I can find your room?"

*This dumb bitch!* I said to myself as I felt Brandon push his gun deeper into my back.

"London Bridges," I said, pissed off at the fact she tried to play me like I was coming on to her. The bitch was ugly as fuck anyway, if I were into girls, she would not be my type.

"Girl, stop it! What is your name? I have too many people waiting behind you, and you are up here playing games."

Once again, I repeated, "London Bridges."

"Ok, next!" she yelled out trying to move on to the next person.

"Look bitch, her fucking name is London Bridges, now give her the fucking room keys before I beat the fuck out of you," Brandon said through clenched teeth, stepping close up to the counter so no one would hear him.

She started typing on the keyboard fast as hell and threw me the keys. We got into the elevator and went up to the fourth floor. I was standing there looking at him, and I wanted to shoot his ass all over again. Just thinking about the image of him and Noelle made me sick to my stomach. This is a man I was madly in love with, and at one time, I didn't want anyone but him. He is sexy as fuck on the outside, but the inside he is made up of dirt and shit mixed together.

The elevator doors opened up, and I felt like I was back in the same position I was in with Justin. What is it with my ass hiding out at hotels and getting snatched up?

"Open the door and don't try no more of that shit you just tried to pull at the front desk. Good thing that lil' bitch was stupid as hell."

He pushed me into the room and made me sit down on the bed as he sat on the chair right across from me. He started scratching his head with the gun before he spoke. "You really tried to kill me London; I thought we were better than that."

"Nigga! Are you on crack? Did you forget you were sleeping with my best friend— not a random chick but my friend, Brandon? Then the fact that you used to mention all the time how she slept around with any and everybody only so yo ass could end up being one of the bodies. At that moment, in your office, I hated everything about you. I hated the way I allowed you to come into my life and sweep me off my feet only to fuck over me. I hated that I ever loved you. Right at that moment you weren't shit to me, and yes, I tried to kill you and to be perfectly honest, If I could do it all over again." I paused and looked him right in his eyes. He looked at me and smiled.

"If I could do it all over again Brandon, I would still try to kill yo dirty lying cheating ass."

The smile that came across his face went away quickly. I know damn well he did not think I was about to say anything different.

"You were mad at me for fucking her but was it really that bad that you tried to kill me over it. And I have every reason to be mad at you too because you were fucking Chase."

"You know what, since you want to bring up Chase, do you want to tell me how you know him?"

"No!" he said bluntly.

I just sat there and started shaking my head. He wants to bring up what I did with Chase and not admit that he was buying pussy like he did not have free pussy at home.

"I'm not about to tell you some shit you already know, what's the point? I'm sure Chase wasted no time telling you that I was buying pussy like it was a pick 5 for 20$ at Sunflower. Look, you want honesty, well I'ma give it to you. Honestly, I got tired of you. The sex became boring, the conversations became dry, and I found more excitement in fucking my hand than fucking you. Noelle came and gave me everything I was missing from you. She knew how to suck my dick just how I needed her to, and she knew how to have that pussy ready as soon as I walked in her house. She didn't nag me, she didn't pressure me, and she didn't come home and talk about some snotty nose ass kids all day."

The more he talked the tears just started flowing down my face. I knew things had changed between us but this; this is not what I expected.

*WHAP!*

I stood up and smacked him in the face.

"How dare yo sit up here and brag about how good my best friend was to you. You know what Noelle was? She was a woman of convenience. If you would have lived with her and did the same shit to her as you did to me, she would have done all of the shit I did. Nagged you, called you all the time to see when you were bringing your ass home, and you would have cheated on her too. Stop playing with me like she was the perfect woman. At the end of the day, she is a woman and you fucking her and still married to me would have eventually gotten old to her. Then she would have moved on from you to someone else. You fucked up your good thing for a piece of ass who could give two fucks how shit worked out for you and her."

"Cookie!" He started biting his bottom lip and squeezing his fist together. "If you ever put your hands on me like that again, I'ma forget that you are a woman and beat yo ass."

*RING... RING!*

Reaching for his phone in his pocket, he answered.

"Yea, you outside?" he questioned, making me raise one eyebrow because no one knows I'm here, and I didn't see him make a call to anyone.

"Ok, here we come." He clicked the phone and pointed his gun at me. "Get up and let's go.

"I'm not going anywhere with you Brandon. I swear if I leave out this room I'm screaming the entire way."

Walking over to me, quickly he snatched me off the bed and pushed me towards the door. I stayed quiet until we got downstairs to the lobby area but as soon as I started seeing people. "HEEELP! HEEELP! PLEASE HELP ME!" I screamed out then I felt a pinch to my side, and everything started to fade to black.

# Chapter 23

## Chase

I was pacing back and forth racking my brain trying to figure out where she could be. Coming home this morning and finding her clothes were gone had me about to lose my mind. When I left, we were in a good space, so I don't know what could have happened to make her want to leave me. She complained about me working a lot, but I thought I made it clear before I left that I would be all hers when I came back. Fuck man, where in the hell could she be? We have a lot of people coming over today for our baby shower, and she is nowhere to be found. Her dad left back out a few days ago, so I know he would not know where she is. The last thing I want to do is call him and make him worry.

"Lucinda, did Cookie say anything to you or anyone before she left?" Lucinda is usually my security camera for the things my cameras do not catch. Her lil' old ass does not miss a beat on what goes on around here.

"No sir, I do apologize, but when she left, I was actually in the basement getting clothes out of the dryer. I did not know she was gone until I cooked dinner last night and she never answered when I buzzed into her room. At first, I thought she was just sleeping, so I went upstairs and knocked on her door. When the knocks went unanswered, I got worried and walked in, that's when I saw all of the things she could not fit any more thrown around the room." She spoke in her thick Spanish accent. "I am really sorry, sir. I should have been upstairs with her."

"It's ok; you did not know she would do something like this. You were only doing your job, and I'm not mad at you for that."

I turned and walked out of the kitchen then noticed the security camera on the wall showed someone was at my front gate. Before she could press the button to call up to the house, I had already opened the gates up for her. I was happy she was here early before the other people started to show up. If anyone knows where she could be, it would be British. As soon as I saw her car pull up to the house, I ran outside and practically threw myself in front of the car to make her stop.

"Boy, what's wrong with you? I almost hit yo ass jumping in front of my car like that."

"I'm sorry B, but it's Cookie."

"Oh my god, is she in labor? What's wrong? Where is she?" she blurted out all of the questions at once, stopping me from asking her ass if she knew where she was. I could tell by her reaction she had no idea she was gone.

"I don't know, that is what I wanted to talk to you about. She tells you everything, so you have to know where she is."

"Nigga, you think I would have come over here if I knew her ass was not at home?" She's got a point there, or she could be trying to throw me off. "She didn't leave a note or anything?"

"No! You can tell she left in a hurry cause it was shit everywhere. I do not know what happened or what caused her to leave, but I need her back here with me. I would never forgive myself if anything happened to her. "Before anyone starts to pull up, you might as well go ahead and let them know there will be no baby shower until I find my babies." With that being said, I turned around and did a light jog back up the stairs to get into the house.

I walked in the house and called up my guy at the police station to track her phone. Here I am sitting rocking back and forth just waiting on my phone to ring. Wherever she is I'm going to find her and make this shit right. Whatever I did, I need to know so that I will not make the same mistake again.

RING!

"Hello," I answered the phone on the first ring when I saw his name come up on my phone.

"Aye, I tracked her phone for you, and it looks like she is at a hotel in Boca Raton."

"The fuck! Aight send me the address of the location. Thanks!" I clicked the phone and went upstairs to change then headed out the door.

***

I approached the front desk to ask the lady if she has seen her. The closer I got the louder she got on the phone.

"Excuse me." She held up one finger telling me to hold on while she finishes up her phone call.

"Girl yes, I beat that bitch's ass."

"Don't you see me standing here?" I spat. She was starting to piss me off.

"Yes I do, and you are being very rude. Don't you see me on the phone?" I reached across the counter, snatched the phone, and threw it across the lobby.

"Now again, you see me standing here, and I need to know if this lady is in this hotel," I said, showing her a picture of her.

"Nope, I don't remember seeing her face." She stood back, folded her arms up, and popped a big ass bubble. I pulled out a roll of money and slid a hundred on the counter.

"Her name is London Bridges; can you please check into the system for me?" She grabbed the hundred and started typing on the computer.

"Now, that you mentioned her name. She checked in yesterday with a man but before my shift was over. I saw them leaving out the hotel again. My shift was ending so I do not know if they came back or not."

"And you are sure it was this woman? Do you know what the man looked like?"

"He was sexy." Looking up at her, she had to be the dumbest person ever. I just shook my head. "Here this is her room key."

I snatched the key and ran to the elevator. I prayed the entire ride up to the fourth floor that she was in her room. The elevator doors opened, and I ran down the hall to her room. I put the key in and burst into the room as If I was going to catch her cheating on me. I walked all the way in and looked around the room, but no one was here. Her room key was left on the bed, the bed was still made, but she was nowhere in sight. I left out the room and jumped back in my car. This is really bugging the shit out of me; it's like she sent me off on a dummy mission. She sent me to some damn Boca Raton knowing she would not be there. I tried calling her phone over and over, but now it's just going to voicemail. *Fuck!* I thought to myself. Where could she be?

221

Using the code to let myself in, I pulled up to Tank's house. He was already sitting outside waiting on me.

"Any news?' He asked right when I got out the car.

"Man hell no, No one was in the room, so I just left. I'm fucked up man. You already know what happened the last time she left. I don't want to go through that again. The lady at the front said she checked in with a man, they went up to the room then came back out and left. I'm not sure if she went willingly or what, but I'm sure she could have asked for help. Cookie is smart as hell, so there is no way she just checked in with a man and be calm about it unless she wanted to."

"Don't say that; you know that woman loves you, man. Don't y'all have those tracking devices?"

"Yea, but it only works when they need help. I can't physically go in and track it until they press the button to send out a signal. Basically, it's turned off until the signal is activated then I can find out where she is and hear her surroundings. That's why I am starting to think her ass is not in danger. She has not pressed her shit yet."

He passed me the blunt, and I just sat there trying to figure out, what I could have done wrong. I have been a damn good man to her. I make sure she has everything she needs and wants. I spend time with her and make sure I show her that I appreciate her. Now, I know lately I have been working and going out of town a lot, but I always come right back to her. That was not an issue before so why now?

"I know you have your own issue going on right now. But, you remember the other day when I asked to see your security footage?"

"Yea the day when Brit, tires got slashed, right?"

"Yea that day, I left out the house in a hurry because I did not know what to tell British. When I looked at the camera, I saw my ex-wife Latoya outside, and she poked a hole in each tire. When I saw her face, I couldn't believe it."

"Wife?"

"Yea, I never told anyone because we basically got married for the money and that's it. I used to have those dreams a lot more back then, and she couldn't handle it. One day I woke up and she was gone. I have not heard or seen her since then, and that was damn near four years ago. We never officially got a divorce because I never knew where she moved to."

"And you have not told British any of this?"

"No, when she asked me about the camera, I just ignored her and told her I would send someone to fix her car, and we left it at that. Well, I left it at that, she still brings it up."

"So that chick Toys, is your wife? I knew it was something about her ass I didn't like. She just showed up out the blue trying to be Cookie friend and bodyguard. It started out with her saying she was paid by that bitch Brandon to kill her."

"In the military, she was a trained sharp shooter. The bitch was bad as hell, and that's what attracted me to her. I don't know what she is doing here, but once British find out she gone lose it."

"Get that shit handle bruh. I'm about to go home. Hopefully, Cookie shows back up soon." I dabbed him up and headed to my car.

# Chapter 24

## British

I could not believe what I just heard. To hear Tank is married already had me furious. I wanted so badly to go out there and curse his ass out. That bitch Toys is the one who fucked my tires up. I told Cookie it was something about that bitch I did not like. It looks like I have to pay her a little visit. I turned to walk away from the door once Chase left. I did not want him to know I heard him and wanted to see how long it was going to take him to tell me the truth. He came back in the house like nothing was wrong. By this time, I was in the family room watching TV. he came in and sat right beside me.

"Did Chase find out where my cousin is?"

"No, he's about to lose his mind. Now he is thinking wherever she is, it's where she wants to be since she hasn't used her tracker or anything."

*RING… RING!*

"Hello." He got up off the couch and took the call into the other room. "Send it to my phone now, and I will handle the rest. Good looking out." Coming back into the room, he grabbed the remote and started flipping channels.

"Who was that?"

"Just Chase, he wanted me to go check something out for him." His phone beeped indicating a text came through. "I will be back shortly; I'm about to go and handle something right now."

Kissing me on my cheek, he then grabbed his keys and left out of the house. I grabbed my keys and left out right behind him. I always know when his ass is up to something, and I will find out. Chase just left so why would he call him instead of telling him while he was here.

I followed behind him for almost thirty minutes before he pulled into a house and got out. I waited a second before I jumped out on bullshit and it was an assignment or something. When he walked on the front porch, the door opened up, and Toys stepped outside. My heart stopped beating when I saw how he embraced her. He went inside, and I grabbed my gun from under the seat and walked my ass right across the street. Tank has me all the way fucked up. This bitch cut up my damn tires, leaving notes and shit on my car like she was gone get him back, and he comes over here like nothing Is wrong. I had something for her ass though. She will not have my man; I fought too fucking hard to let him just leave me like this.

Walking on the porch, I snatched the front door open. Tank was sitting on the couch like everything was cool, he jumped up when he saw me. Then Toys came out of the kitchen smiling with milk in her hand. I didn't even give that bitch a chance to speak or pull a gun on me before I started shooting her ass.

*POW! POW! POW!*

Once I saw her body hit the floor, Tank charged at me, and my reflex caused me to jump, and I shot his ass too.

*POW!*

"Shit British, put that fucking gun down!" Tank spat.

"Mommy… mommy! Wake up, mommy. You said we were going out for ice cream today. Get up, Mommy!"

228

My heart dropped into the pit of my stomach when this little boy ran out of the back room. He looked like he couldn't have been no more than three years old. Tank was standing there holding his arm. The bullet only grazed him, so he was ok; I was not trying to shoot him. I was only shooting the bitch who wanted to steal my family away, the bitch that left him and never looked back. However, when I saw the little boy, I had so many regrets. He looked exactly like Tank, and the look on Tank face lets me know that he never knew that little boy existed.

The little boy walked over to me while I was still holding the gun. He looked right up at me. "Did you kill my mommy?"

I didn't know what to say to him, my heart was pounding so hard, and the tears were threatening to escape my eyes. I didn't want to lie to him, and hell, I didn't want to be honest either, so I just stood there.

"No lil' man, mommy is not dead. She's just playing a little sleeping game. Go back in the room and grab some clothes for me okay. You are going to live with me for a little while?"

"Is my mommy coming?"

"Maybe, I don't know how long her sleeping game will last. Do me a favor go over there to her, give her a kiss on the forehead and tell her goodbye."

"But mommy said never say goodbye always say see you later."

"Ok lil' man, go ahead," Tank spoke to him. He walked over to her slowly and did as he was told before going into his room for clothes. Right when he was out of our sight, Tank stood up quickly and turned to me.

"British, what the fuck is wrong with yo stupid ass? I told you I had something to handle; you had no business following me. You are really starting to get on my nerves with that shit, B. Fuck! You make me wanna knock yo ass out some times," he said through clenched teeth and a tight fist.

I just stood there with tears in my eyes not knowing what to say. Tank has never yelled at me before. I couldn't even bring myself to say anything back to him because I knew I fucked up.

"Take him home now, and you take care of him until I get there. I have to clean this mess up you made. We will discuss this more when I get there."

I think he must have noticed me holding back my tears. I was repeatedly biting the corner of my bottom lip, while they trembled with fear. He looked at me and pulled me into his chest.

"I know you had no idea he was here, I didn't even know he was here, but you have to be more careful, British. You are so quick to pop off without asking any questions. Stop crying, and I will see you when I get home. I'm still mad as fuck at you so don't think shit sweet cause I hugged you. Dry those tears up and woman up."

Moments later, he ran from the back with a little Spider-Man suitcase and a backpack.

I kneeled down to him to be at his level. "Hey buddy, do you have everything you need?" I asked, trying not to let any tears fall in front of him. I knew I fucked up just looking over at her lifeless body and looking back at him.

"Yes ma'am" I grabbed his suitcase and his hand, and we walked back to my car.

After I had made sure he was strapped in, we pulled off. "Hey, little man, what's your name?"

"Tremaine O. Williams, but you can call me Tre."

"Well Tre it's nice to meet you, I'm Miss. British. Are you hungry?"

"Yes ma'am, my mommy was taking me for ice cream after dinner, but I guess she was too tired and went to sleep. But it's ok she can take me tomorrow," his little squeaky voice said.

That instantly made me feel even worse. I do not know what made me do something like that without talking to them. For all I know, he could have been coming over to let her know he didn't want her ass. It's just when I saw him hug her tight, so I knew he missed her.

They have way more history than he and I have, so I wanted to do whatever I had to do to keep my family together. Toys came into our circle from the door with lies. If she would

232

have just been honest, said why she was really here and that she had a child by Tank, things would have gone differently. She brought all of this on herself, yep! This is all her fault.

I was trying to think of anything just to make myself feel better, but the more I looked in my rear view mirror at Tre, the shittier I felt.

We pulled into Chuck E. Cheese, and his eyes lit up like a fat kid in the candy store.

"Yaaaay, Chuck E. Cheese, Chuck E. Cheese!" he chanted over and over until we made it to the door.

I ordered him a pizza and watched him play. Tre is the spitting image of Tank from the shape of his head, to the way he walks. He really is his daddy's son.

"Miss. British, can you come here please, I want you to take a picture in the booth with me. My mommy and I have to take a picture every time we come to Chuck E. Cheese." I forced a smiled across my face for him and jumped up with excitement.

"Let's go little man; I would be happy to take a picture with you." I grabbed his hand and went over to the booth.

We took at least five pictures trying to make sure they were right. On the final picture we were sitting there smiling at the camera, then a head popped on the screen next to Tre that scared the shit out of us both— it was Tank. Right when he stuck his head in, the picture took. He picked up Tre and helped me out of the low sitting seat. The picture fell down the shoot, and I looked at it and smile. Our first official family photo was so cute. Tre and Tank had that same smile going on, and Tre had his arms wrapped around my neck, with his face pressed up against mine.

***

Tre and I walked into the house with his bags. I took him upstairs to his room, which will be right across from ours. He came right into the room, turned the TV on, laid on his stomach with his feet in the air and his head propped up in the palm of his hands.

"Let me know if you need anything." I kissed him on the forehead and turned to walk out the door.

"I just need you to call my mommy, Miss. British," he said never taking his eyes off Spider-Man. "Is my daddy back yet?" When he asked that question, it kind of shocked me because Tank never knew about him.

"He is on the way, sweetheart. Tre, how did you know that was your father? Was that your first time seeing him?"

I know I was wrong for questioning him, but he was a very intelligent three-year-old.

"My mommy shows me pictures of him all the time. I have never seen him before, but mommy came into my room and told me he was on his way to see us."

Standing back up from the bed, I walked towards the door. "Press this button right here if you need me." I showed him the intercom button that goes directly to my room or downstairs.

"You couldn't wait to ask me those questions, B?" Tank questioned, making me jump. I didn't hear him come in or I probably would have asked his ass.

"Sorry, he mentioned his daddy, so I had to ask how he knew."

"Come in the room so I can talk to you for a minute." He turned and walked into the room, and I closed the door behind me making sure Tre could not hear our conversation.

"I still can't believe you did that shit. I thought I was the one with the issues, but no you have issues that yo ass ain't been diagnosed with yet. You gotta be bipolar and have three different people living inside of you or something. I know what it is. You listen to the crazy bitch sitting on your shoulder more than the other bitch that's got sense. You just can't say, nah I'ma trust him, huh? Yo ass goes way off the fucking deep end. All that damn killing ain't cute."

He really was pissing me off, and I refused to stand here and let him keep blowing up on me.

"I need someone who gone listen to me."

What did he say that for? I stuck my fingers in my ear letting him know, nope nigga, wrong bitch. I ain't listening to shit if I feel my gut telling me something is wrong. Nope FUCK THAT!

"What's the fucking difference between when you do it and when I do it? We're still taking someone life, right? So you can stop it with that bullshit you talking!" I spat and started pacing the floor back and forth.

"Oh, you wanna know the difference between what we do? MONEY!" He got close up to my face. "I get paid for my shit while you do this shit cause you scared of someone taking your family. If you scared of that, then stop fucking doing shit to push me away. If you can't trust me, then we can end this shit now. You can keep all this shit." And with that, he got up and walked out the room.

# Chapter 25

## Tank

I jumped into my car after I got the call from Chase with the address and phone number of Toya. I called her up right when I got it, the first and only thing I said was we needed to talk. I was not going there to creep or anything I wanted to let her know even though we never signed divorce papers it has been over for years. She can't just pop back up into my life after leaving me for so long. I had no idea she would never come back home to me.

She pulled one of those tricks fathers used when they wanna leave their family. The bitch said she was going out for milk and never returned. I don't know if I was pissed at the fact she left me, or more at the fact that she didn't bring the milk back because I had my mouth set on some Cinnamon Toast Crunch.

When I pulled up to her house, I couldn't front like I didn't smile just a little bit at seeing her. Toya has always been beautiful to me. Even after all of this time, she kept herself up like she always has. So yes, I picked her up and gave her a tight hug. You better believe once I put her back down on her feet I asked her ass where was my milk. We both laughed and went into the house.

She offered me something to drink, and I accepted. While she was in the kitchen, I was sitting there trying to wrap my head around what I wanted to say to her. I knew I would ask for a divorce because my heart is with British now. Yes, I will always have love for Toya but let's be honest, we entered this marriage for the money. We were never in love with each other; we just had love for each other.

When British burst through the door, I damned near shitted a brick. She had the coldest eyes, and I knew she was out for blood. I don't know what made me not tell her where I was going when I left the house. I guess I forgot I was engaged to a police dog cause her ass can sniff out shit when stuff does not feel right to her.

Before I could ask her to let me explain, she had already let three rounds off on Toya right when she came out the kitchen with my milk. I was in disbelief, not knowing if I should run to Toya or to British. Needless to say, I ran towards British and got my ass

239

shot too. It was only a flesh wound so I would live, but seeing the blood flowing from Toya body lets me know that she would not.

A little squeaky voice came from the back and ran up to her. The little guy looks just like me as a child. My mouth dropped open because I had no clue Toya ass was pregnant. She had better be lucky British killed her ass because once she told me we have a son together, I would have killed her ass, not because of the son, but because she made me miss three maybe four years of his life.

What killed me was when he walked up to British and asked if she killed his mommy.

I did not know what to say, so I lied, I didn't want him to hate British because her ass is about to be the one to take care of him for the rest of his life. I just hope and pray he get this memory out of his head.

"Hey buddy, what are you watching?" I asked as I entered his room and laid down on the bed right next to him.

"*Spider-Man.*" He snuggled up closer to me.

"Hey lil' man, tell me something about you?"

240

"Like what?"

"Anything you like."

"Umm well, my name is Tremaine O'Ryan Williams, Jr. I'm 3 ½ years old. My birthday is December 25, and then I'll be 4. Umm, oh, I have a little sister or brother on the way. Mommy told me this morning, so that's why we were going out for ice cream. She wanted to celebrate me being a big brother soon. Is she still sleeping?"

As I sat there and listened to him talk, I couldn't do anything but smile at how smart he is. I hate the fact I missed so much of his life, having him on Christmas would have been one helluva gift. Then I really just sat there and took in what he said. Toya was pregnant. I know if she told him then she told someone else too. Eventually, someone will come looking for her. Shit! Now I have to figure this shit out.

"Yes, she's still sleeping... she was very tired." I didn't know what else to say, I hate having to lie to him, but I had no choice. I was trying to protect British how my brother always protected me when I fucked up.

241

"Ok Daddy, maybe she will wake up soon."

He shrugged his shoulders and leaned his head on one of my shoulders. After watching a few more episodes of *Spider-Man*, I heard a cute little snore coming from him. I eased his head on the pillow, kissed his cheeks and walked downstairs.

British was in the kitchen fixing her something to eat. She turned to talk to me, but I kept walking out the door. I just couldn't deal with her right now. I walked outside and went into my man cave to smoke a blunt. It's crazy how life can change in the blink of an eye.

*** 

"Grab some things lil' man; we are going to visit grandma and Auntie Cassie, I'm sure they would love to meet you."

He grabbed some clothes, and I did the same. British was still in the bed sleep, and for the moment, I'm good on her. My life has already been fucked up, and I've been trying to get myself back to normal, but her ass is causing more bullshit. I know I do more than tell her I love her ass, I show her too. Nothing is enough though. You know sometimes a person is broken beyond repair, so there's no showing them you are different because in their eyes you are just like all the rest. I know I put her ass through hell, multiple hospital visits and she stayed down with me, but my shit was uncontrollable. Her shit is different.

"I got my stuff daddy," Tre said as he walked into the kitchen with his Spider-Man suitcase.

"Good, let's go." Grabbing his hand, we headed out the door.

I don't know how to explain to my mother that I have a three-year-old son and I'm married, well I guess I shouldn't say married since I'm a widow now. She has always treated me like shit for some reason, and that has always bothered me, but I never said anything. I just hope when she sees Tre she'll welcome him with open arms instead of treating him like me.

We rode through the city until we pulled up at my mama's house.

"Come on lil' man." I picked him up from the back and walked in the house.

"Ma, where you at?" I yelled, walking in and looking in every room until I finally saw her sitting out by the pool.

"Hey, my baby!" She stood up and walked over to me. "And who might this be? He's so handsome." She squeezed on Tre's cheeks. "Come with me. Do you want to get in the pool?"

"Yes, ma'am," Tre replied.

"Oh cute and respectable, I like that."

She took Tre back inside the house and changed his clothes he came running back out with his Spider-Man trunks on and Spider-Man goggles. I didn't get a chance to ask him if he could swing before he did a cannibal into the water then started swimming.

"Whose child is that, Tremaine?" I paused for a second before I answered her.

"He's mine, Mama."

"YOURS? Now you know you are not well enough to have kids. Take that little boy back to his mama and whoever his father is and quickly! Before you do major harm to that child."

"Ma, I'm not taking him anywhere, and what in the hell do you mean I'm not well enough? Every damn time I see yo ass you always talking bad about me. What have I ever done to you besides buy you this big ass house, that BMW outside, who bought that shit? I guess I wasn't capable of it then either, huh. You're lucky I don't put yo ass out this motherfucker with yo bad credit having ass. Now I was gone see if he could stay here until I come back from handling some business, but since my name is on this house and only my name, that means I ain't gotta ask yo ass shit. Tre is staying here until I get back, and you're gone treat him like he is your grandchild, which he is. Now whether you like it or not, we're all gone have to adjust to having him around."

She just sat there looking crazy. I'm tired of her treating me like I'm down bad— especially how she did me that day in front of British. That shit was fucked up.

"Come on Tre, baby. Let's go get something to eat."

245

She turned away from me after looking at me like I was a bum on the streets and helped him out of the pool. I hate I had to talk to her like that, but she needed to hear the truth. You wouldn't have any of this stuff without me. So humble ya self, Ma!

# Chapter 26

## Chase

It's been a week since Cookie left me and I've been so fucked up behind it. Calling her phone is pointless cause it's just going right to her voicemail now. I'm more worried about my babies than anything. She missed her appointment the other day, and that's not like her. I was trying hard not to stress over shit and have faith that she will come to me, but I couldn't help but think about her ass though.

Wondering if she's eating, drinking enough water, taking her prenatal vitamins, or most importantly if she's thinking about me. I miss the sweet smell of her pussy. I miss her perfume. How her hair always smells like fruits. I miss how she tilts her head to the right, fold her arms, and make this cute little expression that she think scares me when I piss her off. I miss when I'm having a bad day she walks in and flashes me that beautiful smile and my whole day would change around.

Since London came into my life, everything has been perfect. I've been picturing the rest of my life with her, and now I'm sitting here trying to see how I'm supposed to live without her.

Resting my head back on my chair in my office, I inhaled and exhaled my Cuban cigar, blowing smoke, making little O's in the air trying to see how I could turn them into hearts how they do on TV. I was enjoying my alone time until a knock came and pulled me from my thought.

*KNOCK... KNOCK!*

"Yea!" I spoke out, trying to see who was at the door.

"Hey boss man, I figured you would be in here. The girls and I are about to go. We made sure we cleaned everything back up, and all of the guests are gone," one of my workers said as she's stepping into the room.

"Ok, just lock the door behind you."

"You ok, boss man?" she asked, closing the door all the way behind her.

"Yea, I'm good, just worried about Cookie and my babies. This shit has been bugging me. I don't know if she's hurt, or if she went willingly since she didn't use her tracking device. Everything is just all fucked up. That shit so backwards we were supposed to be able to track them even if they weren't in trouble but Common's ass picked up the wrong shit. It's been seven days since I've held her, rubbed on her stomach, kissed her soft lips." I closed my eyes and starting trying to picture her face.

"She will be back, don't worry. Let me pour you a drink." She went over to my bar and gave me a shot of Patrón. One shot led to several shots for the both of us. The more I drunk, the more I started thinking about my family. Taking another shot, I had to shake my head side to side because that one made the room start spinning.

"Lean up a little bit boss man." I sat up in my chair, and the next thing I felt was her hands on my shoulders giving me a massage. "You're so tense, stop worrying so much. Cookie is a big girl I'm sure she's not in any danger that she can't get herself out of."

The more she talked, the more relaxed I got. That shit was feeling so good. Cookie used to do this every day I came home. Her touch feels exactly like hers. I closed my eyes again and started trying to imagine it was Cookie. I wanted it to be her so badly, I threw back another shot, and she kept massaging, but this time she started working her way towards my back. My eyes started rolling to the back of my head, and all I could think about was Cookie hands running all over my body. The liquor started to set in more, and after that last shot, I was too fucked up.

"Damn, Cook!" I whispered. I could feel her touching me. I started smelling her perfume, feeling her hair moving by my face, a sweet scent of fruits went up my nose.

"That's right; tell Cookie how you like it."

The gentle touches went from my back to my zipper where she slowly pulled my dick out and dropped down to her knees. Running my fingers through her long soft hair, she started bobbing her head up and down on my dick.

"Shit baby, I've missed yo ass so much. Please don't leave me like that again."

250

"I promise I won't." She spoke into my dick like it was a microphone. "Cum for mama."

She started licking up and down the shaft of my dick. This shit was feeling good; my baby always knows how to please her man. Looking down at her face, she looked so beautiful. I couldn't do anything but thank God for bringing her back home. She looked right in my eyes and flashed that beautiful smile of hers and nut started shooting everywhere. I felt her get off her knees and straddle me. Her pussy was so wet, and I couldn't wait to get deep inside her.

"Hmmm you like that, daddy?" she questioned and continued to ride my dick slowly letting her juices run down my shaft like the Nile River. I love when she is riding me, and I rub on her stomach and feel my babies inside of her. I reached my hand around her stomach, and my eyes instantly popped open when I felt nothing.

"What the fuck man, shit! Tonya, you gotta get up." I moaned out.

Seeing her sitting on top of me instead of Cookie pissed me off. I wanted it to be Cookie so bad; the liquor started playing tricks on me, and I swear I thought it was her.

"Shit, stop! I can't do this; you know Cookie would kill us both." She ignored me and started sucking on my ear lobe, and my dick felt like it was growing larger inside of her.

"She does not have to know, just lay back and let me take care of you. You know you have wanted me for years, don't fight it."

Everything in me was telling me this shit was foul and as bad as I wanted to push her off because she wasn't who I thought she was, my hands felt like they were weighed down with bricks and I couldn't move. She got up and laid on the desk. Her pussy was dripping wet. The good man in me wanted to put her out, but the pit bull that roamed in his backyard is ready to hunt. *Man, this is fucked up,* I said to myself as I stood there stroking my dick.

"Fuck it!" I said aloud, spreading her legs open.

I started sucking on her clit, slowing licking up and down the folds of her lips. Using two fingers, I sucked them and slipped them right inside her pussy and started playing in her juices while I feasted on her like she was some dressing with tons of cranberry sauce on Thanksgiving. Coming up, I slid my dick back inside of her and started knocking down her walls like I was the police. I haven't felt a warm pussy in a week, and after this nut, I promise it won't happen again.

"Ooooh shit, that feels so good, fuck me Chase!" she yelled out.

I instantly started to worry because I didn't want anyone to hear her. I opened my top drawer, pulled out a pair of panties Cookie left one day after I fucked her here and stuffed them into Tonya's mouth. Her screams were throwing me off, and that was all I had to shut her ass up.

Her shit was so tight and wet it kept gripping my man like she was trying to make sure I stayed deep inside of her.

"I'm about to cum." Pumping her faster, she wrapped her legs around me, as soon as I felt my nut coming I pulled out and came on her stomach. The look on her face showed me she was pissed, but I know she knew I was not about to nut in her ass. She got up and went into the shower inside of my office. If she were my baby, I would get in with her, but I'ma let her do her. I have to get dressed and figure out how I gotta make sure she keeps this shit between us. The shower water went off, and she stepped out and grabbed a towel to dry off, making sure she turned her ass to me as she bent over to dry her legs off. I felt my man getting hard again, so I turned around quickly. I didn't want to get myself in any more trouble. She came over and started putting her clothes back on.

"Don't worry; I won't tell anyone that you got that dope dick and you made sure you plunged all of it inside of me."

A chill went up my spine when she said that, and I knew I had fucked up.

\*\*\*

Pulling into my driveway, this funny feeling started to come over me. I sat in my car, and I started to pray like my grandma Alsie Mae taught me.

*Lord, I know you think I only come to you when something is wrong, and I want and desperately need you to fix it. I may not get on my knees and pray to you nightly, but I make sure I say thank you for waking me up this morning. Every morning, that's the first thing I say. That should count for something when I ask you this big favor. My family is missing, and I just need a sign to let me know they are ok. You blessed us with two healthy babies growing on the inside of her, and I know you want them to be with me so I can take care of them how you created me to.*

*Lord, I need you now more than ever. My grandmother always said, "Son, if you pray don't worry, and if you worry don't pray." And I do believe that's how things work, so I'm leaving this all up to you and pray that you lead me to my family and that they are unharmed.*

*Help me, Father. Amen.*

Stepping out of my truck, I felt a sense of peace come over my body, and I knew then that everything would be ok.

"Good morning Mr. Williams," my butler Jesus said once I walked into the house. "It's a loud beeping sound coming from
255

your office. It has been going off for an hour now. Lucinda tried to go inside and turn it off, but the door is locked." When he said that I ran to the office because I could hear the tracker going off, which is the sound he was hearing.

"Lord, please let this be London," I said aloud as I unlocked the door to the office.

Sitting down in my chair, I pressed the remote to pull down the projector style TV from the ceiling. Once it came on, my heart dropped. It was Cookie's tracker going off, and the tears just started flowing uncontrollably. "Thank you, Lord!" I called out to him.

I grabbed my phone and called up my brother and Common.

"Bruh, I'm about to send an address to your phone, meet me there ASAP, and bring your tool bag."

"I never leave home without it." He clicked the phone, and I rushed out the house headed to the address.

The more I looked at the address on the GPS, the angrier I grew. Swerving in and out of traffic, I did the dash all the way there. I spotted Tank's car a block away, and I parked right behind him and waited on Common to pull up.

Once he got here, I briefed them on the tracker for Cookie coming from this house. We grabbed our shit and headed inside.

# Chapter 27

## Cookie

"Brandon, why are you doing this to me? I know I tried to hurt you, but you hurt me first. I was in a moment of rage, and you both didn't give a damn about me. Just please let me go, and I promise not to let Chase kill you."

I have been stuck in Charmaine's basement for a week now. It wasn't until a few days ago that he tied me up because I kept trying to escape but this big ass stomach would not let me get out of the window. I was trying to do anything in my power to get away from him. They would get sloppy drunk in the basement and sit right in front of me and fuck all night. I couldn't do anything but shake my head at the sight of them. I could not believe he was doing this shit. She made sure she kept her eyes trained on me the entire time she was fucking him. Her fucking him wasn't making me mad, the way the bitch was staring at me was.

Once she leaves out the next morning, he would make his way down the stairs and walk me to the bathroom upstairs so I could shower. He would force himself on top of me, and I just lay there and let him do his business how Celie did in *The Color Purple.* I cried plenty of silent tears because I knew if I didn't let him fuck me, then things could end up badly for my kids and me.

The first time he started making me have sex with him, he literally beat my ass because I told him no, tied my hands to her bedpost, and started eating my pussy. The only thing I could think about was the way he was eating Noelle's pussy, and anger filled my body. I was pissed all over again, and my pussy instantly dried up. That shit only made him madder, and he would hit me again.

I prayed I had my cow whip with me at that moment because I promise you we would have been going back and forth with the licks, but I was going to light his ass up way more.

*SMACK!*

"Fuck you mean you won't let Chase kill me. Bitch, I'm going to kill you and Chase and those bad ass kids that's growing inside of you too."

I could feel the blood running down my nose and dripping on this ugly ass gown they made me put on.

259

"Brandon, I want you to hear me and hear me well. When I get out of this, you will die, and sweetie, trust me when I say that is not a threat. I promise you, matter of fact, I pinky promise you, that I'm going to make sure you go meet your side bitch in hell. I told you the last time I whooped yo ass with that cow whip that it would be your last time putting your hands on me."

He let out a loud laugh before speaking. "You thought that would scare me, bitch you are damn near eight months pregnant, tied up to in a basement. You thought that little threat would put fear into my heart. I tell you what I'm about to get out of here and find Chase and kill his ass first. Then I'm coming back for you, so you just hang tight, my sweet sugar cookie because when I come back, it's your turn. I'm tired of playing this game with y'all. It was fun while it last, I thought he would come in like a thief in the night a long time ago but it seems like he doesn't care about his family." He pulled his gun out and cocked it back. "See you soon." He spun around on his heels and left out of the basement. The tears started rolling down my face, and all I could do was pray.

*Lord, I have been praying to you for a week straight, and I need you to work a little faster for me. I know you have a lot to do, and my prayer may not be at the top of your to do list, but Lord, please help me. I know I cannot get out of this without you, I have tried and kept getting pulled back down. Lord, just please send me a sign, something letting me know everything will be ok. My granny is a wise woman from Mississippi and her favorite saying is "If you pray don't worry and If you worry don't pray." I trust you Lord, and I need you.*

*Help me, Father, Amen.*

My babies started moving around and kicking in a way that I haven't felt before.

A sharp pain ran from my stomach all the way down to my wrist making me grab it to massage the pain out. I felt something hard as I massaged it.

"The tracker!" I said aloud and started pressing it continuously. "Thank you, Lord," I said as I pressed on it over and over.

I was praying Chase was at home to hear the alert going off. After a while, I started to get tired of waiting and drifted off to sleep.

"Baby, baby, get up." I could hear Chase, and I just knew I was dreaming. "Cookie, baby."

I felt my arms being freed. I opened my eyes, and there was my baby, Tank, and Common standing in front of me. I threw my arms around Chase, and he kissed my cheeks over and over again.

"Baby I have missed you so much," he spoke between kisses.

"Aye, sis, I ain't trying to break up this little reunion but where's that nigga at?" Tank spoke up with two guns in his hands.

"He left, said he was going to find Chase and kill him then come back to kill me."

"Well it looks like we are right where we need to be then," he replied and reached one of his guns to me. "When this nigga comes back in, we're gone light his ass up like fireworks on the fourth of July, sis!" They cocked their guns back, and Chase put on a cocky stance that made my pussy started jumping. He looked so damn sexy, and he was ready to go to war for his family. No questions asked.

"What happened to your lip?" Chase lifted my chin with his hand towards him.

"He hit me."

I saw him bite the bottom of his lip and anger came all across his face. He pulled me in and gave me a tight hug while rubbing my stomach.

"I'm sorry baby; I should have been here for you," he whispered into my ear right before we started hearing the door knob turn.

He turned around and pulled me behind him.

"Your bitch ass boyfriend is in a good ass hiding spot because his ass was nowhere to be found. He lucky because this was going to be his last day living."

He continued to talk as he walked down the stairs until he got to the last step and had a full view of all of us standing there with our guns raised up at him. "Oh shit!" he yelled and tried to run back up the stairs.

We started unloading all of our clips on his ass. Once we finished, he was laying at the bottom of the steps barely hanging on to life. Tank made sure that didn't last long, he pulled another gun out of the back of his pants and sent another shot right through his head.

"Now let's find Charmaine because I have been waiting to peel her muffin cap back blue!" Tank stated, causing all of us to fall out laughing. This nigga is crazy as shit he always talks about British and I watching too much TV, but this nigga watched too much Kevin Hart.

He jogged up the stairs, and we all followed behind him.

\*\*\*

It feels so good to wake up in my bed again. My pillow top king size bed is the best place on earth right now. I've been sleeping on a military cot for a week, so anything is better than that. Most importantly, I am happy to be in Chase's arms again.

Everything has been so fucked up, and I don't even remember why I left anymore.

I rolled over to wrap my arm around Chase, but when I reached over to him, he wasn't there. I sat up on the bed and looked around. The floor was surrounded with tons of flowers and bags from Jimmy Choo, Christian Louboutin, Michael Kors, Coach, Vera Wang, Louie, and Pandora. I got out of the bed and read the card that was attached to one of the flowers.

*I'm sorry I couldn't protect you, and I promise to spend the rest of my life trying to make it up to you. I'm out running some errands, but I need you to be dressed by seven. I have a surprise for you. Your day will get started soon so be ready. Your driver will be outside waiting to take you to your first stop.*

*I love you London Bridges-Williams.*

I don't know what I was thinking when I left him. Chase has been there for me since day 1 and has done nothing to make me think he was cheating on me. My crazy ass packed up, missed my baby shower, only to get snatched up by my ex.

I started moving around to get prepared for my day then I thought about my cousin British. I haven't been able to talk to her. Dialing her number, I was so anxious to hear from her— that was until she answered the phone all hysterical.

"Hey, cousin," she spoke through constant sniffles.

"Aww baby, what's wrong?"

"Tank, he has not been home in days, and he took little Tre with him. His phone number is disconnected, and I'm about to lose my damn mind."

"Ok just calm down! First question, who the fuck is a little Tre?" Cause that shit had me more puzzled than 100 pieces.

"His son!" she exclaimed followed by a big cry.

She took a deep breath and just let it all out at once. "Turns out that Toys is Tanks wife, that's who cut my tires and left the note on my car. I followed him one day, and he went to her house, and when I saw him hug her, I lost it. When he went inside the house, I followed with my gun, and as soon as I saw her, I shot her. Then all of a sudden a little boy ran from the back, up to her asking

266

her to wake up then he asked me if I killed her; I couldn't answer because I was stuck. Tank made him go and get his clothes packed up and made me take him home after he got there we talked, and he left I haven't heard from him since."

She let out another deep exhale. I'm sitting here holding the phone trying to take all of that in. I didn't want to believe 99% of what she just told me, especially the part about Tank having a son already.

"Well damn!" I finally spoke. "So she really was still on some sneaky shit. I'm glad you killed her ass then. I was wondering why she was staring at Chase the first time she saw him. She must have recognized him from somewhere. I'm sorry you have to go through this. Stop worrying because Tank is fine I just saw him yesterday."

"Wait, I have been blowing you up for a while now, where have you been?"

"I left Chase because I thought he was cheating on me. I got gas at the store around the corner, and I'm guessing that is where Brandon got in my back seat at. That nigga had me locked

267

in a basement for a week. I forgot all about the tracker until yesterday. It's been hell cousin, but I'm glad to be home."

"Yo ass owes me 300$ for all that shit I bought for your baby shower too. You could have at least told me where you were going. Don't ever leave me in the dark like that again, cousin."

"I promise I won't baby. I'll see you soon though. I have to get dressed right now. I love you."

"I love you too."

I clicked the phone and started getting dressed it was already 8:30 so now my ass is up in a rush. I threw on a black, Pink jogging suit with my black Huaraches. My hair was in its natural curly state.

"Ms. Bridges, your car is outside," Lucinda stated as she saw me coming down the stairs.

"Thank you, when I get home please have me some banana pudding made, I've been craving it."

"I made it last night." She winked at me and reached in for a hug. "I'm so glad you are home. That man had been going crazy without you here, and that little girl has been here spending a lot of time with him."

"What little girl?" I asked as I pulled away from her."

"You know, Tonya. I guess she was handling some things for him, but she started getting a little too close for comfort. I prayed to the good Lord that you would come home soon before she had that man doing Lord knows what with her. But don't you fret every time I saw them he was on his best behavior and constantly talked about how he couldn't wait for you to come home."

"Thank you, Mrs. Lucinda."

"No problem, baby girl."

I grabbed my purse and headed towards the car that was waiting for me.

We started out at a massage parlor, then to the hairdresser where she washed and straightened my hair. He had everything planned out so smoothly and for the entire day, I was feeling like a queen. As we continued to ride around the city making stops here and there for jewelry, shoes, and a dress, for some reason what Lucinda said kept playing in my head. I made a mental note to ask him how often she had her ass in my house while I was not there. He was supposed to be out looking for me not entertaining her hoe ass.

Pulling back up to the house, he helped me get all of my bags out of the car. Lucinda had a bowl of banana pudding sitting on the kitchen table waiting on me.

"Thaaank you so much, I needed this because my stomach is growling. Do you mind making me a casserole before I go to dinner tonight with Chase?"

"It's already in the oven."

I'm starting to think she is reading my mind. She winked at me and walked out of the kitchen. I grabbed my bowl and walked into my bedroom. Looking at the clock, it flashed 5 p.m., so I decided to lay down and take a quick nap. After taking one last scoop of my banana pudding, I was out for the count.

# Chapter 28

## Chase

Sitting at the bar with Tank and Common, I was trying to drown myself in liquor. Nothing I did was taking the thoughts and images of me sleeping with Tonya out of my head. I never meant for that to happen and I love the hell out of my girl. I promised her I would be so much better than Brandon and here I am fucking up. When she came into my office at the warehouse, I should have turned her away, but the drinks had me lit. Everything she did started to remind me of Cookie, and I found so much comfort in talking to her. Her smell, her touch, her kisses, everything felt like Cookie. Or was it that I wanted it to be her so badly I was willing to see anything at that moment. At that moment I needed to be deep inside of my fiancée, like a clogged up toilet just plunging the shit out of her.

"Bruh, if this bitch asks you one more time what else you want to drink I'ma smack the shit out of her. Please answer her ass!" Tank spat, pulling me from my thoughts.

"My bad, G. Yea, give me a Tom Colins." I threw back the shot that was in front of me and waited on my next drink.

"Chase, you finally got your woman back home with you, and you're out here turning the fuck up with me instead of being home with her. What's good?"

"Yo lady is at home too, so why are you riding me like that?"

"Touché, she is at home, but that lil' motherfucka is in time out until she gets her shit together."

"Nigga, how are you gone put somebody in time out. Both of y'all crazy so y'all might as well be crazy as fuck together and live that crazy happily ever after life together."

"Fuck that! She crazier than me, and I thought that shit was highly impossible." He chugged his beer down and ordered another one.

"Take now for instances I bet she is tearing the house up pissed because she hasn't heard from me in days. She blew my phone up when she noticed I was gone after I dropped Tre off at mama's house."

I know he caught the side eye I gave him when he mentioned our mama. They have not been on good terms in years, so I found it very strange that he even ran to her. Hell, I would have just stayed with B, then deal with mama's ass.

"Oh you already know she tried me, and I had to let her know that all this shit is in my name so she might wanna tread fucking lightly with all that bullshit she was talking." I took a sip of my drink and a deep breath.

"Bruh, if you about to start crying I'm about to go," Common spoke up and said to me.

"Cry? Fuck you think I am. I may be fucked up right now but I ain't down bad. This shit is fixable. All I had to do is come clean to Cookie and let her know what I did."

Tank rubbed his hand over his face. "You've got to be one of the dumbest niggas," Tank huffed. "Why would you tell her you fucked another bitch? Unless yo ass plan on doing it again, that

273

shit would go to the grave with me. She should definitely understand that the floor was slippery and you slipped into another bitch pussy. End of story." He started cracking up laughing. "Nah, I'm joking. Sis is gone fuck you up if she finds that shit out, though. I'm not in a position to give advice so I'ma sit here and help you drink until you come up with something."

"Me too," Common chimed in.

Neither one of these niggas is worth a damn. I'm about to go home and get ready for this date I got planned for Cookie. Looking down at my watch, I threw some money on the bar and headed for the door. I told Cookie to be ready by seven and here it eight p.m. and my ass ain't at home yet.

*Fuck, she's gone kill me!* Jumping into my car, I headed towards the house. I pulled my phone out of my coat pocket and saw I had 30 missed calls and 30 messages. I didn't even bother to read them; I will just deal with it when I get home. I already know she's about to let my ass have it.

Using my finger to open the gates that lead up to my home, she was sitting outside on the porch waiting for me. I got out the car and ran up to her apologizing for being late.

"Baby, I'm so sorry, I lost track of time. Why aren't you dressed?" She was sitting outside with her face full of makeup and tears. I noticed that once I finally got a good look at her. "London, please don't cry. I'm sorry, baby. Please let's just get dressed and enjoy the rest of the night. I wanted to take you dancing and to dinner."

"No, I'm ok! You can go. I'm not really up for doing anything anymore. I'm tired, these babies are having a wrestling match with my bladder, and I can't stop pissing on myself. I just want to ball up in my bed and sleep."

"Ok, and I will ball up right next to you. Whatever you want me to do baby, I will do it."

I stood up and helped her up from the swing, and we walked into the house. Following her up to our bedroom she climbed into bed, and I hopped in the shower. Washing my body up a few good times just to get the liquor smell and smoke off me from the bar, I got out and headed into the room with her.

"Baby did you fin—" I cut my sentence off once I noticed she was asleep already.

Getting into bed with her, I pulled the covers back and started planting soft kisses all over her stomach. I've missed her so much. An entire week without having her next to me had me all fucked up. I started working my way down, leaving a trail of kisses from her stomach to her ass cheeks.

Palming one in my hand, I spread her cheeks and started making love to her ass with my tongue. She started squirming letting me know she was waking up. Rolling from her side to her back, I got on my knees, pulled one leg up, and kissed from her ankle up to her inner thighs.

Letting out a deep sigh of pleasure, I could see her kitty was soaking wet. Putting her leg over my shoulder, I stretched my body out completely and just laid there eating her pussy until she came over and over again. Her legs were shaking uncontrollably, and my face was covered in her juices. Leaving one last kiss on her

276

kitty, I came up and laid beside her. Wrapping my arm around her, I started hearing the soothing sounds of her light snores. When I placed my hand on her stomach, my boys were moving like crazy. I couldn't do anything but smile because I was happy my family was home with me safe and I promise not to let them out of my sight again.

***

Getting up the next morning, I decided to run around outside to clear my head. This shit with Tonya is really bugging me. I feel so bad. I'm not that guy, and I have never been that guy. The last thing I want or wanted to do was hurt my baby. I haven't seen Tonya since that day, and I'm glad too. I know being around her will be strange as hell. I'm not sure how Tonya will act with Cookie now either. Regardless of how Cookie acts all sweet and shit, she is still British's cousin and has some crazy tendencies inside of her too. Tonya will come up missing before I know it.

*RING... RING!*

I pressed to answer on my Bluetooth once I saw it was my brother.

"What's good?" I answered, trying to catch my breath.

"Meet me at the hospital now!" I heard my little sister screaming in the background, and he clicked the phone. I rushed back up to the house and grabbed my keys. Forgetting to let Cookie know where I was going, I just jumped in my truck and did the dash to the hospital. I made it right when Tank and Cassie pulled up.

"What's going on, bruh?" I saw tears rolling down Cassie's face, so I pulled her into my chest.

"It's mama, she was at the breakfast table this morning and all of a sudden she started grabbed her chest and slumped over," Cassie cried into my chest.

"It will be ok sis, let me go inside to check on her." Pulling away from her, Tank and I walked inside of the hospital and left Cassie sitting outside on the bench.

"My mother Cheryl Williams just came here by ambulance. Can you tell us what room she is in please?" I asked the receptionist. She looked up from her phone and rolled her eyes.

278

"She's not in a room yet."

"How would you know if yo ugly ass never even looked her fucking name up?" Tank spat, and I already knew he was about to lose it.

I sent British a text asking her to come up here because she seems to be the only one who can calm him down when he gets like this now.

"Look, don't come up here with all that. I said she is not in a room yet so have a seat!" she exclaimed as she stood up and gave Tank a stern look and smirked her lips at him.

I don't know what she did that shit for because that nigga was about to smack her so hard her lace front was gone lay back down cause that shit was coming up.

"Bitch, you're lucky I don't hit women and my girl ain't with me or ya ass would be back there waiting on a room with my mama."

"Go walk it off, bruh. I will handle this."

I turned and spoke to the receptionist "Look, I really need you to go back there and see what's going on with my mother. Her name is Cheryl Williams, and she just pulled up maybe 5 or 10 minutes ago." I slid her a $50. She looked at it and pushed it down in her bra before walking away.

I waited at the counter until she came back. I looked outside to see if Cassie was good and I saw her crying into some nigga's arms with long ass hair. Tank must have spotted her too because he was headed out the door.

"Ah, fuck!" I ran out after him.

"Get the fuck off my sister. Cassie get yo ass in there and check on mama."

"No, I'm good right here."

"Oh, fruit booty here is gone make sure you are good?" Tank yelled out, making dude step to him.

"Fuck you call me?"

"Is the sugar in your tank clogging up your ears, my nigga? I said, is fruit booty gone make sure she's good?" Whoever dude was he reached back and knocked Tank on his ass.

"Yea nigga, you big but yo ass fall hard. Don't ever come at my girl with no bullshit like that. If you got an issue with me, then you come to me as a man. Other than that, I advise yo ass to go check on yo mama cause I got this right here."

British came running up to Tank to help him off the ground as soon as he said that. He jerked away from her and walked back inside of the hospital, but not before yelling over his shoulder.

"Cassie, ya nigga fucks boys in the ass."

*** 

After waiting in the waiting room for hours, a doctor finally came out to talk to us.

"Is the Williams family here?" We all quickly jumped up and ran to him. "Hi, I'm Dr. Kevorkian, and I have been attending to your mother since she came in. She suffered a massive heart attack."

Thinking the worse, Cassie immediately started crying. Dude with the long hair stood up and pulled her to him. Tank's eyes started blazing with fire.

"Not right now, bruh," I whispered and put my arm around his shoulders. "Go ahead, Doc. We're listening.

"She suffered a massive heart attack, and one of her lungs collapsed. We now have her in a medically induced coma. You guys are more than welcomed to come in to visit her, but only one person at a time for right now. She won't be able to respond, but they say even in a coma they can still hear you talking, so you guys pull it together and help your mother get through this. The lady at the front desk will let you guys back when you are ready."

He turned away and Tank and I just stood there trying to take all of this in.

"I will go back first then you and Cassie can come after," Tank spoke up and walked to the door. The lady he just cursed out stood there and watched him and still didn't open the door for him.

*SMACK!*

"Bitch, don't you see my man trying to get back there to check on his mama. Do your fucking job and press the gah damn button!" British yelled out.

"I told you!" Tank said to the lady and started laughing. Even when he and British aren't on good terms, they still rock with each other hard, and I love that shit.

# Chapter 29

## British

After trying to reach Tank for days and days, my ass fell into a deep depression. Nothing has been right without him being with me. To the ones on the outside looking in, we aren't right for each other, but I know this man was made for me. God made him fearless, and he made me strong. Whatever he goes through in life, I was designed to make sure he stands 10 toes down and not let the fact that he feared nothing get him killed.

I was so happy when I got that text from Chase telling me Tank needed me. When I walked up to him on the ground, all I wanted to do was rushed to him and make sure he was good. When I did that, he made sure to let me know he wasn't fucking with me. Snatching away, he made his way inside the hospital. I know this was the wrong time to be thinking of this, but the way his white button down clinged to his muscles had a bitch in heat. He left the first few buttons open revealing his tattoo on his chest.

"Sis, not right now!" Chase spoke, shaking his head at me. He must have seen the way I was looking at Tank cause I swear I wanted to ask his ass to cash me in the bathroom how bout dat!

"Leave me alone, I wasn't even thinking anything," I lied.

I was thinking how I couldn't wait to get him alone so we can have crazy makeup sex. These babies have my ass horny as the fuck lately, and that damn toy ain't been helping me at all. I can't work that toy like I can work Tank.

I looked over and saw Cassie smiling at the cute guy with the curly hair. She looked so happy with him. Watching her, I couldn't do anything but smile.

"Hey Cassie, I'm sorry to interrupt but have you seen Lil' Tre?"

"Yes, we dropped him off with our cousin before we came up here."

"Is there a way you can call her and let her know I will be coming to pick him up?"

I wasn't thinking about nothing Tank said. I fucked up and killed this little boy's mother, and the least I could do was raise him. He didn't need to be dropped off when he has a big ass house and yard to play in. Since he has been gone, I have been working hard as hell making our home more kid friendly, and I cannot wait to see his reaction.

Walking into the hospital, I saw the lady at the front desk just standing there looking at Tank wait on her to open the door. That shit instantly sent heat through my body. I laid that bitch lace front down when I smacked the fuck out of her. I don't know what she thought this one, but I'm the only bitch that plays with that one like that. She was in the right damn place for me to lay hands on her ass too. Tank ole ignorant ass started laughing at the lady, and she quickly pressed the button to let him back.

"Aight, they gone put yo ass out of here!" Chase chuckled.

"That's cool. I'm about to leave anyway. I see he really does not want me here, so I'm going to pick up Lil' Tre and take him back to the house. Tell Tank I will see him later if he asks about me."

286

I reached in and gave Chase a hug because he looked like he needed it. From Cookie to his mama, this man is gonna break down sooner or later.

"Don't stress, everything will work out in your favor. Remember, if you pray don't worry, and if you worry don't pray." His eyes lit up like the Christmas Tree in Rockefeller Park when I said that.

"My grandmother used to tell me that all the time."

"Mine too, very wise women I see. So you don't worry, just let God handle all of this. Tell Tank I will see him later." I waved bye to Cassie and left out of the hospital. My first stop was to pick up lil' man and take him to the house.

***

"Thank you for picking me up, Miss British." Lil' Tre spoke once I got him seated in his booster seat.

"Not a problem lil' man, I wanted you at home with me anyway. Ooooh and when you get home, I have a big, big surprise for you."

"I love surprises, Miss British," he said in his soft monotone.

I think it's so cute how his voice doesn't change. He's excited, but you can never tell, just like his father. That man knows he can hold some emotions in. By the time we made it half way down the street, I looked in my rear view mirror, and Tre was already knocked out. I drove to McDonald's to grab him something to eat then headed home.

"Wake up Tre; it's time for your surprise." He woke up with the biggest smile on his face.

"Is it in my room?"

"Yep go right up, and I will be there in a moment."

He jumped out of the car and ran inside. I could hear the pitter patter of little feet racing up the stairs. I waited until I heard his scream before I went inside. I knew he would be extra loud when he saw his room. Making my way in the house, I followed the screams up to his bedroom.

"Oh thank you, thank you so much. I have always wanted this, and my mommy always told me it was too much money. I'm glad she's not here she would be a mean mommy at times, Miss British. If I did something wrong, she would always yell at me and say, *Get out my face looking like yo damn daddy.*" I had to hold my laugh in at him trying to mimic her voice.

"Sweetie, don't say that. Your mother did all she could to be the best mother she could be to you. She was doing it all alone too, so be thankful for the things she did get you. But, as of now go in and enjoy your room."

He ran back inside and started jumping on his bed with his Spider-Man comforter on it. The walls were painted blue and red with white spider webs, with Spider-Man painted on top of a tall building. Oh, and I had to make sure I put his name on the wall too. He had stuffed spider men here and Spider-Man action figures there.

"I have one last surprise for you, Tre."

"Dang Miss British, what I do so special. It's not my birthday… is it?"

289

"No baby, it's not your birthday yet, but I just wanted to shower you with gifts for all the birthdays we missed."

He wrapped his arms around my legs and gave me a tight hug. I grabbed his hand and led him outside to his large Spider-Man inflatable bounce house. His eyes lit up, and he ran over and started jumping when he saw that. I pulled up a chair and watched as he wore himself out.

"Thank you for taking him home with you," Tank spoke, causing me to jump.

"Daddy, daddy, daddy!" Tre screamed and ran over to him. Tank kneeled down and caught him, kissed him on his forehead, and told him to go back and play.

"This is really nice, British. This will take some time for all of us to get used to, but I want, well I need you to stick by me through this, especially since yo trigger happy ass fucked up. Did you know she was pregnant?" My mouth dropped open. As if I didn't feel bad already I feel even lower now.

"How'd you know?"

"Tre told me the other day, that's what they were going out for ice cream for. So they could celebrate him being a big brother." Tears started to fill up in my eyes. He pulled me into his chest and started rubbing on my head.

"I have been calling your phone nonstop, Tank. I really wanted you guys home with me. I didn't know where you took him and your mother does not like me, so she was the last person I was going to call. You left me in this big ass house alone. Why is your phone saying it's disconnected."

"Because it is, I changed my damn number on yo ass and got a new phone. I ain't for that stalking shit. That's how your ass ended up getting shot the last time because you don't know how to listen and hang tight."

"And that's how yo ass is still standing up here today because I was on my stalker shit and saved your life," I intervened.

"See that's what I'm talking about, you can never just shut the fuck up and listen. Just trust that I got us and won't do anything that would cause friction in our relationship. I want you now more than ever. You are the mother of my kids and will soon be my

291

wife. Just trust me, B." He leaned down and gave me a long deep kiss.

My pussy started getting so wet that I almost forgot Tre was outside and pulled my dress up on his ass. This pussy needs some attention, so Tre's lil' ass is going to bed early.

# Chapter 30

## Cookie

It's been a whole day, and I have not heard from Chase. I have been blowing his phone up nonstop, and it is going right to voicemail. You would think his only priority right now would be to be home with his family. He already had my ass waiting to see him all day yesterday and came home after it was time for us to go out for dinner. I sat there and ate that entire casserole Lucinda made, and it was good as hell too. He comes walking his ass on the porch like I was really about to go out with him. His ass came home and jumped right in the shower. Now if that shit didn't look suspicious.

Here it is now 11 p.m., and I still have not heard from him. I grabbed my iPad, pulled up my Kindle and started finishing up *Love and War: A Hoover Gang Affair* by Latoya Nicole. She is a bomb ass writer and all her shit be crazy as hell. I swear her character, Gangsta from her book *Gangsta's Paradise*, reminds me of Tank's foolish ass. I sat down on my swing outside and covered up in a throw cover my granny made me when I was a kid and started to read. The hours passed by and I started to feel myself drift off.

As I stood up to stretch and walk inside the house, I saw some headlights coming up the driveway. I turned and started back walking in the house. I was not about to let him even think I was sitting outside waiting on his ass. Even though I was, his ass does not need to know that. I took my robe off and got in the bed only to pretend I was asleep.

He came right inside and turned on the shower. Once he got done, he laid in the bed with his back to me and knocked out. That shit pissed me off for real. I slid out of bed, walked into the bathroom and closed the door behind me. Chase never picks up his clothes out the bathroom, so my ass is about to see what he been up to all damn day long. I kneeled down on my knees and started with his shirt. I pulled it up to my nose and took a big sniff. The smells of perfume caused me to grow even angrier. But, I wanted to give him the benefit of the doubt, so I over looked that and kept on sniffing until I made it to his boxers. I picked those up and looked around the bathroom like someone was watching me, even though I had the door locked. I did not want to risk anyway seeing me sniffing on my man draws like I have a fucking problem.

Pulling the boxers up to my nose, I inhaled deeply and smelled nothing but shit. It smelled like this nigga been passing gas none stop in the seat of these damn draws. The fuck this nigga been eating refried beans or some shit. Fanning the smell away from my nose, I got up and got back in the bed with my back to him.

"They smelled good, huh?" Chase mumbled and went back to sleep.

I wanted to bust him in the back of the head when he said that shit. My ass must have sniffed hard as hell for him to hear me with the door closed. Stuffing the pillow between us with an attitude, I rolled on my back and went to sleep.

\*\*\*

"Good morning, Lucinda," I spoke upon entering the kitchen. She smiled and pulled the chair out for me at the table that was filled with everything that I love to indulge myself in.

"I hope you have plenty of room because it's just you eating this morning. Mr. Williams grabbed a few pieces of bacon on his way out the door."

"What time did he leave?"

He was really starting to piss me off with this shit. The late nights and early mornings were getting old, and he don't even say, baby, I'm gone, I will see you later or shit like that. I could feel the tears threatening to escape, and I quickly wiped them away.

"It was around 6 a.m., I just started cooking, and he grabbed the little that was there and left out the door."

She fixed my plate but all of a sudden, I didn't have an appetite anymore. I started to feel like I was back with Brandon again. A million and one things were running through my mind. I nibbled on the food so that it would not go to waste. I grabbed me a bowl of fruit that she had on the table and went upstairs to his office.

Taking a seat in his chair, I started popping grapes in my mouth while my eyes scanned the room. I was not sure what I was looking for, but I was just curious. My eyes continued to roam the room until I spotted the camera on the wall above his bookshelf. I pulled the screen down from the wall and started looking at the footage, mostly focusing on the time I was not here. British came by a few times, and so did Tank. A few of the girls stopped by the office and chatted for a little while then they left, but that damn Tonya was seen on several different videos always trying to be the last one there with him.

I couldn't find anything on the cameras at the house that was out of the ordinary, so I pulled up the one from the warehouse where he has his meetings with the girls. Going back to a week ago, I searched and searched. Every camera, every angle, every room, my ass was in there like Inspector Gadget. I must have searched for 30 minutes nonstop before I came to last Friday. He must have had a party for the girls to meet some new guys there. There were bottles being popped, asses being shook, and breasts being shown. As the party starts to wind down he remained in his office while the girls cleaned up and to my surprise here comes Tonya knocking on his office door.

I turned the audio on so I could hear what she was saying. The more she talked, the more pissed I got, but it seemed to relax him. She kept giving him shot after shot. Even Ray Charles could see what she was doing. This bitch is trying to fuck. I guess she thinks her pussy is special because she doesn't fuck with the men she only does dates. There's no way Chase would fall for this shit. He is too smart of a man to be finessed out his dick like that.

Moments later I heard him call out my name while she was massaging his back and this hoe had the nerve to reply like she was me. Ain't that about a bitch. He took another shot, and I could tell by the look on his face that he was lit.

"Lord, please don't let him fall for this stunt," I said aloud and started back looking at the camera. "Don't do it, baby, don't do it," I chanted.

She dropped down to her knees and pulled his dick out and started sucking it like she was in a bad bitch contest and she wanted to be in first place. The tears started to fill up in my eyes, but this time I did not stop them from falling. I let them escape as I sat there and continued watching. He reached around her stomach

298

like he does with me every time I ride him so that he can feel my stomach. Once he realized it wasn't me I thought for sure he would stop. Then I heard this nigga say, "Fuck it". That was all I needed to see and hear.

"I'm done!" I said aloud and stood up from his chair making sure I left the video on the screen and paused on the part he was eating her pussy. This is definitely Brandon all over again. I prayed that Chase was different, but he really proved to me that all men are the same. Heading upstairs and just as quick as I packed the last time, I packed even faster this time. I refused to cry over this because I should have known better. It was my fault for trusting him and moving with him so quickly. I deserved this shit right here for being so fucking stupid. Continuing to throw clothes in the bag, I grabbed my keys and walked out the door.

Turning my music on, I blasted Mary J Blige's "Not Gon' Cry". I sang along with her with tears streaming down my face.

I know there are no guarantees, in love you take your chances but some how it seems unfair to me. Look at the circumstances, through sickness and health, till death do us part. Those were the words that we said from our hearts.

Brushing the tears away I turned the music off and focused on the road. With no destination in mind, I rode around until I got tired of driving.

Pulling into Starbucks, I parked my car and went inside. I could feel my phone going off over and over again, and each time I looked at it, it displayed Future on the screen. I pressed ignore one last time before I powered my phone off.

"How many I help you?"

"I just need a bottle of water and two of those double chocolate cookies."

Taking a seat in the far back corner where I didn't expect anyone to find me, I pulled out my phone and powered it on, only to call up British.

"Hey, baby," she answered on the first ring.

"Hey cousin, can you talk?"

"For you? Always! Let me go outside." I heard her tell Lil' Tre she would be right outside if he needed her.

"I'm here boo, what's wrong?" I started boo hoo crying, with the ugly crying face and all when she asked that question. I couldn't fight those tears any longer. I was fucked up inside all over again.

"He cheated on me!" I exclaimed, grabbing napkins off the table to clean my face.

"Nooo Cookie, please don't tell me that."

"I wish I didn't have to tell you that, but it's true. I watched the tape."

"Bitch, that nigga did not make a sex tape!" This made me laugh a little because she always goes to the extreme.

"Girl no! The cameras in the warehouse. He fucked Tonya, and lately, he has been…"

"Wait! Hol' up, hol' up… he fucked who?"

"Tonya."

"Your worker Tonya? The Tonya that acts like her pussy is pure gold, and she don't fuck nobody Tonya?"

"Yep, that bitch fucked him like she wanted to be in my shoes bad. But it's cool, even if it just happened one time. That one time was enough for me. I have been down this road before and he was right there with me when I went through the shit. So, he knows firsthand on the bullshit I went through already. He is just a different nigga with the same lies. Anyway, I will call you and let you know where I am. As of right now, I'm just here at Starbucks sipping on water until I get sleepy."

"Ok baby, you call me if you need me and please don't leave me in the dark. Wherever you decide to go tonight call me and let me know, regardless of the time. I love you."

"I love you more." I clicked the phone.

Right when I looked up, it was this fine ass man sitting at the table next to me. I sat in this corner for a reason, and it's 10 empty seats in here, and this nigga decides to take a seat right next to me. Giving him a fake smile and quickly turning my head, I know I was looking bad as hell with tears rolling down my face, but for some reason, he kept looking at me and smiling.

"May I help you?" I finally spoke up.

"I saw you over here crying, and I wanted to make sure you were ok. A woman in your predicament should not be out here crying." I frowned up before I knew it.

"Fuck you mean, in my predicament?" I spat.

Holding his hands up surrender style, he replied, "I apologize, pretty lady, I should have said that differently. I'm sure you do not need to put any stress on the kid you are carrying. That's the predicament I meant. I'm sorry for saying it wrong and taking you off of your throne. You came off that thang quick ready to fuck me up." He laughed and sweet baby Jesus, I was having a flash back on the first time I met Chase.

This man that was standing before me was truly God's gift to woman. I couldn't tell how tall he was because he was sitting down, but I could tell his body was sculpted to perfection.

He wore these gray sweat pants, a white polo t-shirt that was so tight it looked like it was checking his blood pressure. Long curly lashes surrounded his chinky eyes, with skin smoother than a bitch edges after she just got a fresh relaxer. His complexion was so perfect— like milk chocolate with just a hint of vanilla mixed in. He had a mouth full of perfect white teeth and a smile that would melt the heart of even the coldest woman. One of his arms was covered in tattoos. It's just something about a man with nice art work on him that makes my knees go weak.

"No, I apologize. I've had an extremely long day. Actually a day from hell. I can't say it was the worst day in my life, but it's definitely in the top two."

"Whatever he did to you, I hope he can fix it because you were over here crying your eyes out. I didn't want to freak you out by sitting next to you, but I needed to come see if I could do something to make your day better. By the way, my name is Adam." He reached his hand out to me; I hesitated before reaching mine back to him.

"I'm London."

"That's a beautiful name."

He gave me that smile again that made me forget why I was crying. I don't know why I'm sitting here trying to look cute and shit like I don't have a whole man at home and not only that like my stomach ain't protruding out.

"Well, it was nice meeting you," I stated thinking he would get up and leave.

"I was hoping I can just sit here until you start to feel better again. God forbid you start crying, and no one is here with a shoulder for you to lean on. You don't even have to say a word to me. You do you, and I will read a book to keep me from staring into your beautiful face. My sister Manda P just dropped this book called Where I want To Be, and I promised her I would check it out. I promise I wont bother you." I couldn't stop blushing for the life of me.

"Sure, it's not like I have somewhere to go any damn way."

"Are you homeless?"

"Nigga!" I blurted, making my neck snap towards him. "Hell no, I'm not homeless, I actually have a big ass house, but I just choose not to be there anymore."

We must have sat there for hours talking about everything under the sun. His last relationship, my last relationship, and shit even the one I'm in now was talked about. I was sitting here laughing and talking to him, thinking the more I talked about it, the better I would feel, but that was a lie. I was still hurting like hell. I wanted Chase to be my forever. There is no way in hell, I can forgive him for cheating and couldn't forgive Brandon. That's my whole thing; I would look like a weak, crazy bitch staying with him after I watched him entertain a female like that. Then for him to actually think about stopping only to go right back in face first, like the thoughts of me was not enough to make him stop.

"I like talking to you, London."

"I like talking to you as well, Adam. You are really keeping my mind off all of the bullshit I'm running away from. I wish I could talk to you all night, but I should be going, so I can find me a place to sleep tonight. It was nice meeting you."

I'm not sure why, but talking to him gave me so much comfort. It's like I was finding peace in a stranger all over again. Certain things he said or facial expressions he made, had me thinking I was looking into Chase's eyes and it kind of fucked me up for a minute.

"If the situation were different I would be asking for your number right now— not the situation pertaining to you being pregnant because I could care less about that. I would be there for them just like I would be there for you. The situation I was talking about is your relationship. If you ever decide to leave him, you should most definitely look me up. I would love to get to know the London behind the tears," he stated, making me once again blush like a high school girl.

I attempted to get out of my seat, but a sharp pain ran through the lower part of my stomach. "Shit!" I yelled out and started trying to rub the pain out of my stomach. It would go away for a little while then come right back. It felt like my stomach was in a tight knot and the pain started to come back to back.

"You ok? You need me to call someone?" Adam asked with much concern in his voice.

"No I will be ok, I just need to breathe through the pain, everything will be juuust fine," I lied.

It wasn't fine because right when I said that, more pains started shooting through my kitty. After that last pain came through it was followed by water coming out of me slowly. I have never had kids before, but I am almost positive my water just broke. I looked down at him and couldn't do anything but laugh at how this stranger was literally on the ground trying to catch the fluid with a cup that was leaking from me so I wouldn't get it all over the floor.

"Adam, please grab my phone out my purse and call my cousin British. Ask her to meet me at the hospital."

Breathing through the pain, I waited until the pain stopped before I attempted to get up. I could hear British screaming through the phone.

"Who the fuck are you?"

"I'm Adam, I just met your cousin, and she is in labor, so instead of asking me questions, you need to be getting to the hospital." She was about to cuss his ass out again, but he clicked the phone on her, picked me up bridal style, and carried me out of the door.

"My car is that way."

"I know, but you can't drive it, so I will take you to the hospital. Calm down, I'm not going to do anything to you, but Maybe after you drop these babies, I will." He winked at me, and through all the pain, I still managed to blush at his extra sexy ass.

He picked me up like I was light as a feather stiff as a board. Laying me on the back seat, he did the dash all the way to the hospital with his hazard lights on. The contractions were getting out of control, and the only thing I could do was moan and hold my stomach.

"Just hold on, we are right around the corner," he spoke trying to keep me calm.

That shit was not working. I needed to know that we were pulling up at the hospital, not that we were around the corner. Taking one last deep breath, I felt the car turn into the hospital really fast. He jumped out of the car and ran inside. Moments later nurses were running out of the door with a wheelchair rushing me inside.

"Are you the father?" one of the nurses yelled out before pushing me through the double doors. He looked down at me and then back at her.

"Yes!" he replied and made his way to the back with me.

# Chapter 31

## Chase

I woke up early this morning to go and sit with my mom. Cookie was sleeping so peacefully I didn't even bother waking her up. On top of it being 6 a.m., she would have cursed my ass out so fast. So, I left and was going to call her once I thought she was up. I made it to the hospital, asked the nurse for a warm blanket and a pillow, I stretched across that uncomfortable ass couch and fell right back to sleep.

Just watching my mom lay there is fucking me up inside. She hasn't always been the best mother to us, mostly Tank. For some reason, she had it out for that man. They are so much alike, but he just looks more like our father, and I think that's what she hates, well dislike most about him. He walks like Pops, talks like him, and hell, he even smiles exactly like him.

When we were kids, daddy came home one day and introduced us to our half-brother. I thought it was weird because he was born right before Tank. He and my mom never separated,

311

never divorced, or anything so how this lil' nigga came about I don't know. But, she welcomed him with open arms whenever he did come over. Once we got older, we lost touch, and I really didn't care because I still only fuck with my brother. Half motherfuckers don't count to me. I think that's why she always fucking with Tank because she is still hurt from the shit pops put her through.

I watched as the nurses kept coming in and out of her room checking on her. I grabbed my phone not knowing it was dead, I put it on the charger just long enough for me to power it back on. I decided to call and check on Cookie, but all of my calls were going unanswered; which isn't like her unless something is wrong. Other than that, she usually answers on the first damn ring. I know she is approaching her ninth month, so I need to keep close tabs on her at all times. Calling her phone one last time I decided to leave mama alone for a little while and run home to check on Cookie, making sure I let the nurse know that I would be right back just in case Tank and Cassie showed up. Getting into my car, I made my way down the expressway to the house.

I noticed her car was already gone so she must be out with British somewhere.

"Hey Lu, where's Cookie?" She turned her nose up at me and kept walking.

Now, I don't know what her problem is, but she's forgetting I'm the nigga that signs her pay checks. She does that shit again, her ass will be swimming back across the water with her no green card having ass. The fuck she think this is.

I headed into our bedroom. When I walked past my office, I caught a glimpse of the TV. My heart started pounding as I looked up and down the hallway before going into my office and closing the door. As I sat there in my chair looking at the TV, I knew then that I had fucked up big time. How could I not remember I have cameras in every inch of my house and warehouse? I don't trust a soul so I made sure I could see everything.

"FUCK!" I roared.

I turned the TV off and walked into our room. Looking around the room, I realized that once again she's gone. After blowing her phone up a million times, I started to grow angry. I understand why she is upset, and she does have every right to be, but this leaving bullshit is for the birds. She never tries to sit down with me and talk shit out. The first thing she does is grab that raggedy ass Louie bag and leave.

I know one thing for sure and two things for certain, I'M NOT LOOKING FOR HER ASS. I'm tired of this shit for real. Tonya was a big ass mistake, I was fucked up, and the shit just happened. It would have never happened if she hadn't left like she just did. She made room for someone to come in and fuck her man. Fuck, this is some bullshit.

I tried to call her a few more times, but after it started going to the voicemail, I stopped trying. I see now that this shit is not going to work out for us. As I walked out of the room, I saw it was something hanging on the bathroom mirror. Snatching it down, I started reading.

*I don't know what possessed me to think that you were going to be different. Chase, I loved everything about you from your head down to your toes. I would NEVER do or say anything that would hurt you to your core like that. Seeing you with her took something away from me. At that moment, I became a heartless bitch. After you, there is nothing anyone can do or say to make me believe all men aren't the same. What hurts the most is you knew what I went through. Hell, you supplied him with the bitches, so you knew how he was out here treating me wrong. You wiped my tears as I cried on your shoulders plenty of nights thinking about how my husband fucked me over. Who's going to wipe my tears now as I cry thinking about how you did the exact same thing he did.*

*I couldn't forgive him, and I don't know how I will be able to ever forgive you. Letting you back in is like me telling people that it is ok to get cheated on as long as they only do it one time. Fuck that; it is not ok. That shit is the worst feeling in the world, and I wouldn't wish this on my worst enemy. I prayed that you were different. I opened up to you too soon, with hopes that you would be there for me and never let me down. You fooled me*

*Chase. I LOVE YOU, and I will call you when it's time for the*

*babies to arrive. As of right now Chase, I'm good on you play boy.*

*Sincerely,*

*A Crumbled up Cookie!!*


I balled up the letter and threw it against the wall. I can't believe she said it was over. She got me all the way fucked up. I went down stairs and headed back outside to my car.

Instead of heading back to the hospital, I made a detour to this little bar around the way. I called up my brother to meet me there so we could talk. Driving up to the place, the images on the TV screen kept playing in my head. My heart dropped when I saw it, so I could only imagine how Cookie felt watching it.

Taking a seat at the bar, I started throwing back shots of Hennessy, again seeing if the liquor could drown the pain I was feeling. I knew I should have just told her the truth, but naw, I listened to Tank's ass knowing this nigga ain't got an honest bone in his body.

316

"What's wrong now? You know you only ask me to meet you at the bar when yo ass done fucked up," Tank hissed, taking a seat right next to me.

"It's all fucked up now, bruh. I honestly think Cookie and I are over for good. She found the tape of Tonya and me."

"Nigga, y'all made a sex tape?" he blurted out.

"Nigga! You've got to be bullshitting me. Do it look like I record a bitch I'm fucking?"

"Well technically back in the day..."

"That shit does not count," I replied quickly. "College days do not count, bruh. Those hoes would do anything to fuck the star of the football team, and back then, I had enough meat to go around. She went through the security footage and saw us in the warehouse fucking. And to make sure I knew she saw it, she left it on pause on the screen. All I saw was my face between Tonya's legs. I know I hurt her, and I was doing so well with keeping her happy. I don't know how I ended up in this shit."

"Bruh, Tonya been trying to fuck you since Hush was a puppy. She ain't out here not giving these niggas her pussy for a reason. She's been marinating that shit just for you. You fucked up when you allowed her to get that close to you. She got way too comfortable, and because you were lonely and vulnerable, you welcomed whatever she had to offer you at that moment. Now you gotta figure out how to get your woman back."

He sipped his drink, and once he was done, he left my ass sitting right there in my feelings.

*RING... RING!*

"Sup, B?"

"Get to the hospital now; Cookie is in labor!" British yelled through the receiver.

Throwing my last drink back, I paid my tab and got on down. I was so happy I was about to witness the birth of my lil' men. Most importantly, I'm glad Cookie wasn't mad enough at me to make me miss their birth.

I jumped on the expressway and hurried to the hospital. I was glad it was a park right up front because my ass was a little tipsy and I did not feel like walking far.

"Hey I'm here to see my wife; she's in labor right now."

"Her name?"

"London Bridges." She looked at me and smirked.

I'm so tired of motherfuckers trying my baby for real. Her name is pretty as fuck and much better than what she was rocking on her work badge. Some damn Tomnesha. I'm guessing both parents couldn't agree on a name, so they mixed their names up together.

"Yo daddy name Tom, huh?" I asked.

"Yea, how you know?" She looked up with the biggest smile on her face.

"Lucky guess. Anyway, have you found my wife room yet.?"

"Yes, she's in room 304, but she can only have one guest in there at a time, and one is already back."

I took a seat and texted British to let her know I was in the lobby and she can come out so I could go in. Seconds later British walked through the door with Tank. A puzzled look came across my face, and I was about to break down every fucking door in this hospital if they don't let my ass back there.

"Aye, can you let me back please?" I asked as nice as possible since this was the same bitch who tried Tank when he wanted to see mama.

British must have noticed her too, she stepped to the counter and when the lady saw her getting close to her, she quickly pressed the button.

Running to the room number, I could hear her screaming and the male doctor telling her to breathe deeply. Pushing the door open, to my surprise there wasn't a doctor in sight. Once I saw him kiss her on the forehead and put some ice in her mouth, I lost it.

"Yo, my nigga, what the fuck are you doing here with your arms around my fucking wife?" I yelled out to my half-brother, Adam.

# TO BE CONTINUED

But wait.. there's more.

Next Series Alert: Sneak Peek

# She Wanted The Streetz
# He Wanted Her Heart

## Chapter 1

### Briana 'Bonnie' Johnson

"Say ma, you gotta minute?" he asked, as he starts to do a slow jog to catch up with me.

As he jogged, I couldn't help but watch his dick bounce from one leg to the next, like it was playing hop scotch. *Does this nigga have on draws?* I thought to myself, that shit was moving around too freely.

"I'm Wayne, but you can call me Weezy," he spoke in a raspy tone.

He smiled at me and I saw his bottom row of teeth was gold and his top was pearly white. He didn't look like the type of man who would be hanging in the streets. He looked more like a house nigga than the ones who would be out in the field. What did he want from me I had no clue. Cause trust me I'm not your average around the way girl. These legs don't fly open for the first nigga that run up behind me.

"I'm Briana, but you can call me Bonnie."

"Hmm." He put his hand to his chin as if he was thinking about something.

"Bonnie and Weezy— that has a nice ring to it."

"Oh, does it really?" I started blushing because this man is all types of fine.

"Most definitely, you mind if I take a walk with you?"

"Sure, I'm just headed home. I just got out of class and need to check on my dad."

"I can dig dat. I like 'em fine and educated. What are you going to school for?"

"Phlebotomy."

I was hoping he knew what that was so I would not have to explain it to him. It's already the beginning of August, so it's hot as hell here in Memphis. He's standing here holding a conversation like we are not in the middle of a heat wave.

"That's what's up; my lil sister is going for the same thing too. I don't see how she can just stick people all day long, but to each is own right!"

"Exactly," I stated, looking down at my watch. "I'm sorry to cut this short, but I really need to catch this bus," I said, turning to look at the bus about to pull up across the street.

"Nah, no shorty of mine about to catch the bus."

I paused as I was starting to walk off. I had to blush cause that shit caught me off guard.

"Let me give you a ride."

I hesitated a little bit, but shit, from the looks of the bus, it was already crowded, and I don't feel like standing up having some fat nigga rub on me and call it an accident. After being in class all day, standing was the last thing I wanted to do. *Fuck it, why not*, I said to myself before turning to walk back towards him.

"Ok, as long as you promise to keep your hands to yourself." He smiled and winked before grabbing my hand and walking me back around the corner.

"I'll holla at y'all later!" he yelled out to three guys sitting on the porch.

He hit the alarm, and when I laid eyes on his car, my pussy got wet. I talked all that shit about not being the average bitch, and I'm sure the average bitch most definitely gave the same reaction I just did.

It was this all black Challenger, not no basic shit— it was fully loaded. And when I got in, I noticed he had two nitro buttons right by his gear shift. It's something about fast cars and a fine man pushing all that horsepower that turned me on.

He closed my door for me and pulled off. I watched him as he weaved in and out of traffic, shifting gears so smooth like it was an automatic. I had to adjust myself in my seat cause I could feel my kitty throbbing. Looking over at him, his wet full lips caught my attention. He had just licked them, and I swear I was sitting over in my seat thinking about what that mouth do. I was doing so well with my celibacy shit, but for some reason, I felt myself about to lose it.

We pulled up to my house and exchanged numbers. I knew he wanted to come in, but I had to make sure my dad was good first.

Two years ago I found out my dad had prostate cancer and it wasn't until a few months ago when they gave him a few months to live. He is only 50 years old, surgery would help him but getting the money was not easy. I've been saving for years, and we still haven't reached the amount he needed. My day job wasn't cutting it, and the night job is giving me the blues.

Stepping into our house, I quickly ran to the back room to check on my daddy.

"Hey, Dad, what are you up to?" I asked, in a worried tone as I watched him stare out of the window with this pitiful look on his face. He still can get around and go outside, but he just chooses not to.

"Hey Bonnie," he spoke. His voice had grown so weak and weary over the years, and it always saddens me to hear or even look at him like this.

My mom died last year from a heroin overdose. She had become so stressed out with taking care of my father. I guess heroin was the only thing that helped her take her mind off of things. It's just my dad and me now living in the house that my parents owned. I work two jobs and go to school. My day job is something simple just dropping fries here and there, but my night job is where I make the most of my money. Even though the job is degrading, it helps cover the medicines my dad need and his weekly visits to chemo. We could have more than what we have, but his shit is draining me dry.

Our house is a nice size, but the upkeep is too much for me to handle alone. After paying for the medicines he needed, I only had enough for necessities. I work hard, and truth be told, I'm tired of living like this. I'm 21 years old, and I can't do anything I want to do because I'm too busy taking care of my dad. Don't get me wrong I do love him, but I love myself too, and lately, I've been neglected. It's always work, school, and home. I rarely sleep because I'm up all night getting this money.

I have always wanted Louis Vuitton luggage, but definitely not under my eyes, and trust me, that shit is far from cute. Looking out the window in the front room, I could see Weezy is still sitting outside, but I had to clean up the house a bit before I let him in. My dad had shit everywhere, on top of it smelling like a damn hospital in here. I had to make a mental note to myself to buy more air freshener.

I grabbed our last bottle of Glade and went crazy spraying the house. I saw my dad sleeping again, so I closed the door and locked it from the outside. He sometimes has a way of ruining relationships for me, coming out the room with his shit bag hanging out. My guest always got turned off and made some type of excuse to leave.

After making sure everything was clean, I walked outside and waved for him to come in.

"It took you long enough," he announced, stepping into the house.

Shit, he looked even better than he did 10 minutes ago. He took his hair out of the bun he had his dreads in, and now they are hanging down past his shoulder. Taking all of him in, I finally stepped aside to let him come all the way inside.

"Yea, sorry about that, I had to make sure my dad was squared away first. He has cancer, so I'm constantly having to do something for him.

"I'm sorry to hear that ma, you ever thought about putting him in a home or something. I know that's yo pops, but shit, the way you got out of class and had to rush home to see about him, it seems like you don't have a life of your own." He sat down on the couch and started staring into my eyes.

"I want to put him in a nursing home so he could have around the clock care, but it's too expensive."

He kept asking me questions trying to get to know me more and pretty much listened to all of my problems. I really thought I was going to talk his damn ears off. The longer he sat there, the more I opened up to him.

"What else do you do besides school and take care of your pops. Do you ever get time to yourself?"

"I work two jobs trying to make ends meet with the bills for the house, and his doctor bills, but we barely have enough to get by. It's becoming a burden on me, and I don't know how much more I can take. I'm starting to stress out, and it's showing with my school work.

I'm trying to make him as comfortable as I can; all the while I'm making myself uncomfortable. It's not fair to me, I sacrifice a lot for my dad, and I just want to live."

I felt him wipe my eyes and pull me into his massive chest. I didn't even realize I was crying. I guess I had been holding all of this in for so long and anyone that shows the slightest bit of interest in what's going on in my life, I just let it all out.

As I laid there with my head on his chest, I could not do anything but take in his scent. He smelled so good, and his hair smelled even better. I don't know what cologne he was wearing, but I'm sure it's called pussy magnet cause it definitely had my ass stuck on him. It's been so long since I have been held by a man, hell it's been so long since I have spoken to a man even this long. Luckily, I locked my dad in his room, or he would be walking out right about now.

"You're fucking with the right one now shorty. Just let a real man get to know you a little better. You seem like a dope ass chick. Ain't too many females out here hustling like you are, and I like that shit. I don't want no woman if she doesn't know how to get bread on her own too. What if one day I'm not here? My lady's gotta know how to survive in these streets."

He keeps calling me his lady, but once he finds out everything about me, I'm sure the lady shit will fly out the window.

We laid there on the couch, and I got so comfortable that I had fallen asleep on his chest. I didn't wake up until I heard a loud snore and saw him knocked out. Looking at my Fossil watch, I saw it was a quarter till 11 p.m., and I was supposed to be at work over an hour ago.

"Wayne… Wayne… get up." I rocked him back and forth trying to wake him up. He woke up looking around like he was trying to figure out where he was at.

331

"My bad ma, I didn't mean to fall asleep on you. I got too comfortable and a nigga ain't had a good sleep like that in days."

He stood up and stretched, and I couldn't help but to give his body a once over again and admired the way his shirt hugged his muscles, and his pole print was so visible, it stuck out even more than it did when I first saw him. Again, he caught me looking at him, so he grabbed his dick and licked his full lips.

"You keep looking at him like you want 'em or something. All you gotta do is say the word ma, and I will have yo lil' thick ass bent over one of this couch calling me zaddy."

He closed the gap that was between us. This nigga had me clutching invisible pearls when he said that shit. It has already been too long, but I'm definitely not about to just hand him the pussy over on a platter. He's gone have to work for this.

"You're silly. I wish you could stay longer, but I am already late for work."

"It's cool, mama. This won't be the last of me you see." He kissed me on the forehead and walked out the door. I watched as he drove away before I went to my room to get dressed.

*Shit... daddy,* I thought to myself, when I walked passed his room door and saw it was still locked. I had been so wrapped up into Weezy that I forgot I had him locked inside his room.

I unlocked the door, so I could peep in and check on him. Once he heard it opened, he turned around so fast and chunked his shit bag at me.

"Yo ass been out there laid up with some nigga and forgot all about me. You will not do that shit in my house. If you wanna lay up, do that shit in your own place. You can get the fuck out, and I mean right now."

I forgot to mention my dad has become so damn evil. As long as the attention is on him, he is good. That's why his ass sits at that damn window all day, so he can see who comes and goes. I can't take too much more of his shit literally. Here I am standing in the door way laced in his shit.

This right here will be the last time I get hit with some shit. The first time, I knew he was just upset, but his ass is making this a habit whenever I upset him. He wants me to leave, cool... let's see how his old ass survives without me.

"There's a special place in hell for you, Daddy. I have been nothing but good to you, put my life on hold to make sure your last days were the best days, but you, you are too fucking selfish to see that shit. Every dime I have made I put it into this raggedy ass house of yours and on your medicine. Let's see how far that lil' check you get monthly take you because I will be damned if I sit here and take care of anybody that treats me like shit. Never bite the hand that feeds you, Daddy. Just know that you will need me before I need you."

I slammed the door and went right to my room to shower. Once I got out, I grabbed as many clothes as I could and left out the house, with no destination in mind. I knew I needed to get to work because now I needed money more than ever. I walked around the block and dropped my clothes on my granny back porch. I was happy she stayed close by because I had entirely too much shit.

After putting my things down, I went right to work. The rest of this shit I will figure out in the morning, but right now, I needed to get to this schmoney.

**\*COMING SOON\***

**She Wanted The Streetz**

**He Wanted Her Heart**

**Please leave a review!**

**Thank you**

CPSIA information can be obtained
at www.ICGtesting.com
Printed in the USA
LVOW10s0121020318
568443LV00007B/55/P